I0609340

Henry Churchill De Mille, David Belasco

# The Charity Ball

A comedy drama in four acts

Henry Churchill De Mille, David Belasco

**The Charity Ball**
*A comedy drama in four acts*

ISBN/EAN: 9783744781619

Printed in Europe, USA, Canada, Australia, Japan

Cover: Foto ©Andreas Hilbeck / pixelio.de

More available books at **www.hansebooks.com**

# -%- THE CHARITY BALL -%-

A

-*- COMEDY DRAMA -*-

IN

-:- FOUR ACTS -:-

BY

-%-DAVID BELASCO and HENRY C. DE MILLE-%-

## -:- C A S T  O F  C H A R A C T E R S -:-

JOHN VAN BUREN - - - - - Rector of St. Mildred's.

"DICK" VAN BUREN - - - - Firm of Van Buren & Creighton, No.- Wall St. known on the St. as "The Earthquake"

JUDGE PETER GURNEY KNOX- Left over from a past era, unable to catch up with the present.

FRANKLIN CRUGER - - - - The King of Wall St.___

MR. CREIGHTON - - - - - Jr. Partner of Van Buren & Creighton

ALEC ROBINSON - - - - - Ambitious to be dubbed on "Change" "Alexander the Great."

MR. BETTS - - - - - - - The Organist of St. Mildred's.

PAXTON - - - - - - - - - Confidential Clerk of Van Buren & Creighton.

CAIN - - - - - - - - - - "A thing of shreds and patches".

JASPER - - - - - - - - - A Servant.

--0--

MRS. VAN BUREN - - - - - The Rector's Mother.

BESS VAN BUREN - - - - - Tired of dolls,ready for beaux.

MRS. CAMILLA DE PEYSTER- Who dabbles in stocks "just a little bit."

PHYLLIS LEE

SOPHIE - - - - - - - - - Maid at the Rectory.

ANN CRUGER.

---0-0-0-0-0---

# THE CHARITY BALL.

## ACT I.

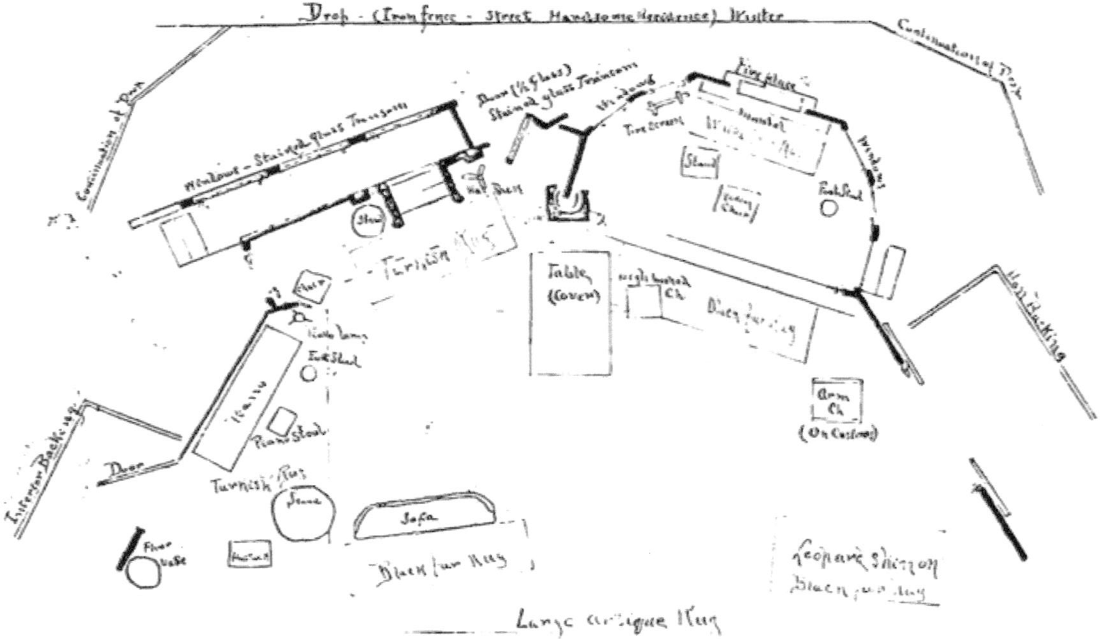

Drop - (Iron fence - Street Handsome Residence) Winter
Continuation of Drop
Continuation of Drop
Window - Stained glass Transoms
Door (½ Glass)
Stained glass Transoms
Windows
Fire Screens
Fireplace
Mantel
Windows
Stand
Foot Stool
Hat Rack
Stool
Turkish Rug
Table (Cover)
High backed Ch
Black fur Rug
Hall Backing
Arm Ch
(On Castors)
Piano Stool
Turkish Rug
Door
Interior Backing
Sofa
Black fur Rug
Floor Vase
Leopard Skin on Black fur Rug
Large antique Rug

Acts 1st and 4th

PROPERTY PLOT --- ACT I.

---oOo---

Ground cloth and Medallion down. Rugs as indicated.

-o-o-o-

FURNITURE REQUIRED: (For arrangement see Diagram)
Large floor vase, (down R.)
Piano and Stool, R.
Sofa, R. C.
3 Stands (R. C. -- Up R. C. and up L. C.)
Hassock.
2 Footstools.
Piano Lamp.
Standing Hat Rack.
Small Table, C.
Small Rocking Chair, in Alcove up L. C.
Fire Screen.
Large Upholstered Arm Chair, (on Castors) L.
High Backed Chair L. of table C.
Light Chair up R. C.

--0--0--

ON STAND, R. C. Table cover, Plush Album (with Photos) Basket to weave. Handsome Vase on lower shelf.

ON SOFA R. C. Large Silk Pillow.

Hassock R. C. with Upholstered Seat.

Piano Lamp up R. to Light. (Handsome Shade)

ON PIANO R.: Scarf, Several Books, Handsome Vase, Music &c.

ON STAND UP R.C. Two or Three Books.

ON TABLE C. Handsome cover.

Cushion on Rocking Chair up L. C.

ON STAND UP L. C. Two or Three Books.

ON MANTEL UP L. C.: Clock, Pair Bronze Vases, Two or Three Small Vases, Six or Seven Books, Matches in Match-box on Small Tray.

Fire in Fire-place throughout Act. Fender, Fireplace furniture, &c.

Arm Chair L. on Castors (To be pushed easily through door L.)

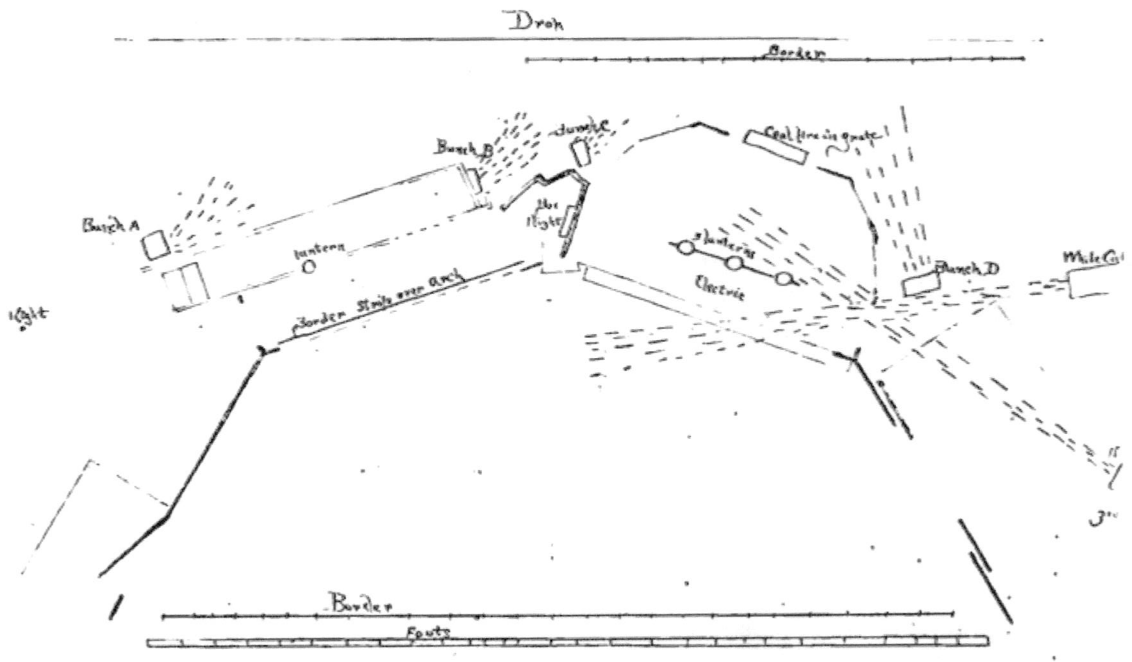


Act I. Gas or calcium.

LIGHT PLOT ------ACT I.

--:0:--

AT RISE OF CURTAIN Foots and Borders on full.
Bunches A, B, C, and D (all working together) on WHITE

ON CUE, "CORK!" Foots and Borders worked down to 1/2 slowly.
Bunches A. B. C. and D. gradually change to Blue.

Lanterns and Box light up C. to be lighted by Jasper.

White Calcium, (from above) L. and Red Calcium also from above, L., to be put on when Phyllis lights lamp. Remain on till curtain.

Fire in fireplace throughout act.

House lights on 3/4 at rise of curtain. Down gradually to 1/2 on cue "cork."

----oOo----

# -%- T H E  C H A R I T Y  B A L L -%-

## -:-A C T  I.-:-

S C E N E: The sitting room at the Rectory. Christmas Day '87. (For arrangement of furniture see diagram.).

D I S C O V E R E D: Mrs. Van Buren on steps L.2.E. listening. She is an elderly woman white haired. She is blind, but moves easily about the room, always cheerful.

Mrs. Van B.

The parish buildings are a perfect pandemonium.

(Sophie enters R. U. E. and comes down the steps laden with a large box of toys and comes down R. C.)

How happy those children are over their Christmas dinner! Sophie, have you the toys?

Sophie.

A few of them.

Mrs. Van B.

(Feeling them) Dolls for the girls and marbles and bats for the boys and - oh, dear! those horrible tin horns. What would an American boy be without his tin horn?

(Bess enters L.2.E. sees her mother, runs quietly round to R. and stands with uplifted face, intercepting a kiss.)

Take them along.

(Exit Sophie L.2.E.)

Child laughter is like an echo from another world. Bess!

(Drawing her close to her.)

Bess.

(Pressing her cheek against her mother's)

Angel!

(Going quickly up C. and looking off R.)

Dinner's over; and Ann is giving out the presents. My! How my heart's bumping!

Mrs.V.B.

(Crossing to sofa R.)

What's the matter?

Bess.

Alec's coming to take all the children.

Mrs.V.B.

(Sitting on sofa R. and weaving basket which she finds on stand R.)

Take them! Where?

Bess.

Take their photographs, angel. He told me this morning he'd come.

Mrs.V.B.

Did you see him this morning?

Bess.

I see him every morning.

Mrs.V.B.

Bess!

Bess.

Accident!

Mrs.V.B.

Every morning?

Bess.

(Coming down to back of sofa)

Nothing more natural. As I go up Madison Avenue to school, he comes down Madison Avenue to business.

Mrs.V.B.

Does he walk all the way to Wall Street?

Bess.

(Coming around and half sitting on sofa on the L. of Mrs. V. B.)

Oh, dear no! He turns back and carries my books for me to sixty-seventh street, and then takes the Elevated. Brother John caught us one morning.

(Kneeling beside Mrs. V. B.)

He knows we are sweethearts.

Mrs. V. B.

Sweethearts! What do you and Alec find to talk about.

Bess.

Lots of things! He's in Mr. Franklin Cruger's office, studying for a stock broker. He hadn't been there a month before Mr Cruger told him he knew more about the business than he did.

(Rising, going up to L.2.E.)

You ought to hear him give quotations.

Mrs. V. B.

Poetry?

Bess.

No, stocks, angel. Why doesn't Alec come? The children are just dying to have their pictures taken.

Betts.

(Heard singing outside R.)

If a body meet a body
Coming through the rye,
Is a body kiss a body,
Need a body cry."

Mrs. V. B.

(Speaks during Betts' song) I do love to hear Mr. Betts dip into the grab-basket of old song and bring out the first he happens to get hold of.

(Betts enters R.2.E. He is a man about fifty, with long white hair, strong characteristic face - the embodiment of joviality. His clothes a trifle eccentric, not exaggerated. He carries a cloak on his arm and a very large umbrella. As he sees Mrs. V.B. and Bess, he ends with a chuckle.)

Betts.

Miss Lee is in the reception room.

Bess.

(Crossing to R. up stage) Miss Lee!

Mrs.V.B.

Did you have any trouble in finding her?

Betts.

Not after Mr. Van Buren's description --"a sad, pale-faced girl." Her face made me think of -
(Hums) "The heart bowed down by - "
Shall I bring the young lady here?

Mrs.V.B.

If you please.

(Exit Betts R.2.E, humming the air "The Girl I left behind me.")

(W A R N M U S I C)

Bess.

(Who has seated herself on hassock R. of stand R. and opened album)

If she is half as pretty as her photograph here - who is Phyllis Lee?

Mrs.V.B.

A young girl whom your brother John met during his visit to Florida. As she was coming to New York, and a total stranger here, he asked me to invite her to remain with us for a time.

Bess.

Isn't that like Brother John?

(M U S I C)

(Phyllis Lee appears at back from R.2.E. in travelling dress, she is almost timid in manner. She is preceded by Mr. Betts.

Mrs.V.B.

Alwats by the side of misery, lifting from despair many a poor creature, whise first happiness was his help and friendship.

Betts.

(To Phyllis) Go to her. She can't see.

(Aloud)

Mrs. Van Buren.

Mrs.V.B.

Oh!

(Putting out her left hand)

This is Phyllis Lee.

(Phyllis com s down and takes her hand.)

(Betts crosses L. and exits L.2.E.)

Bess.

(Bounding to the left of her and seizing her left hand) Oh, I'm awfully glad to see you.

Phyllis.

Madam - Miss Van Buren.

Bess.

Call me Bess. (Kisses her)

Phyllis.

I overheard your words Mrs. Van Buren. Even you do not know what his help means.

Bess.

Well, if you like brother John so much, I wonder what you will think of Dick.

Mrs.V.B.

(Laughs) She thinks there is nobody like her brother Dick.

Bess.

Except brother John. But I must say Dick gives more presents. In his last letter from Paris he promised me a great surprise.

Phyllis.

He is in Europe.

Mrs.V.B.

Yes. He has devoted himself so persistently to business, it has affected his health.

Phyllis.

Not seriously I hope. (Anxiously)

Mrs.V.B.

Unless the Umbria brings a letter to-day I shall feel worried.

(Phyllis slightly overcome, supports herself on table C.)

Bess.

(X'ing to her back of table) Why what's the matter, Miss Lee?

Phyllis.

(Recovering) Nothing - I - . . .

Mrs.V.B.

You must be worn out. Bess will take you to your room.

Phyllis.

Thank you.

(M U S I C)

Bess.

Come along, Phyllis. You don't mind my calling you Phyllis do you?

(Exit with Phyllis upstairs R.C. and off R. chatting)

You see when two girls meet, and like each other right away, the sooner they become acquainted with other, the better. I'm awfully anxious for you to meet Alec Robinson. He's one of the nicest fellows in New York.

(Mrs. Van Buren takes up basket and commences to weave)

(During latter part of last speech, Mrs. De Peyster heard speaking outside R.)

Mrs.D.P.

(Outside) In here? Oh, thanks, I'll find her.

(Enters Mrs.D.P. R.2.E. She is prepossessing in appearance, dressed in the latest fashion. Her manner is brisk and matter of fact.)

(Coming down to Mrs.V.B.) Good morning, dear, good morning. I think after such a busy day's work, I may take a half holiday.

Mrs V.B.

Ah! Camilla.

Mrs. D.P.

(Sitting in chair L. of table C.) I rushed away after service this morning. You see during the second lesson, Mrs. Homer G. Putnam said to me: -- her pew is next to ours you know - that if I held any shares in the Consolidated Gas Tank Co., to get rid of them at once. I had a thousand. I don't know what in the world John preached about this morning. I had tanks in the brain. Just imagine my anxiety. Being Christmas Day, of course, my broker would not be down town. I sent messengers flying in every direction. And where do you think we found him? In a Turkish bath spending his Christmas. But by twelve o'clock to-morrow some one else will be asphyxiated with my gas.

Mrs.V.B.

Back from Europe only three days, and already deep in speculation?

- - -

Mrs. D.P.

Oh, my dear. I've kept my feelings bottled up so long that the moment I landed, out popped the cork.

(Coming down to Mrs.V.B.)

Oh, by the way, how well Judge Knox is looking. I saw him at Daly's last night. He bowed and smiled. I beckoned to him with my fan, but he shook his head. Do you think anything could have induced him to move from that orchestra chair? Not a bit of it. I once said to him, "How is it, Judge, I never see you go out between the acts?" He replied, dear old fashioned fellow, "Madam, though I am not a camel, I provide myself for the entire evening."

(Sitting on Mrs. Van Buren's left.)

While I was abroad I received a letter from him with these words -- "When next we meet, prepare to be astounded." Now what do you think he means?

Mrs. V.B.

It isn't very hard to guess.

Mrs.D.P.

(Divining her meaning) No!

Mrs.V.B.

For the past six months, we have heard nothing from Judge Knox, but Mrs. De Peyster. When did you hear from her. Is she well? When will she return?

Mrs.D.P.

(Much pleased) Really? What else did he say?

(Alec enters C. carrying photographic apparatus, his manner that of a boy verging towards manhood.)

Alec.

(Putting the two packages on floor and leaving tripod against column C.)

Auntie, got three cents for the messenger. I'm just that much short. How 'de, Mrs. Van Buren?

(Going to her and taking her hand, then taking off overcoat and hanging on rack up C.)

Now, Aunt Camilla, don't be all day; these messengers charge by the second. It'll be four cents before you get it out, and five before I can get to him.

Mrs.D.P.

(Who has opened purse and taken out a bill)

Oh, I have nothing but five dollar bills.

Alec.

(About to take it) That will do very nicely, thank you.

Mrs.V.B.

(Feeling in her purse and taking out three pennies.)
I have some pennies here.

Mrs.D.P.

(Returning bill to purse.)
That will do better.

Alec.

(Coming down to her and taking pennies)
Mrs. Van Buren, never do that again. I am just four dollars and ninety-seven cents out.

Mrs.D.P.

Whatever that boy does with all the money he gets-

Alec.

All I get! Six dollars a week salary, and fifteen allowance. If I didn't invest a little in Wall Street, I wouldn't have enough to keep me in neckties.

Mrs.V.B.

Alec, do you speculate?

Alec.

Well, I'm not in Franklin Cruger's office for nothing.
(Enter Bess R.3.E. and unseen by Alec comes slowly down R. watching Alec.)
At first I was a little bit dizzy at the way he'd wipe up the street about once a week. But I didn't lose a point. Every time he took a flyer I flew with him. Every time he dropped I went clean out of sight. I was with him though. Oh, wait till I'm called Alexander the Great, Auntie, you'll be proud of me yet.

(W A R N  M U S I C)

Bess.

(Apart to her mother). Oh, Angel, isn't he smart?

Alec.

Hallo, Bess!

Bess.

Hallo, Alec!

Alec.

Come help me untie this camera.
(They go up the stage and unwrap camera)

(M U S I C)

Ann.

(Outside)
Now, now! Be patient and I'll read you a story.

Mrs. V.B.

There's Ann Cruger.

Mrs.D.P.

Ann here?

Mrs.V.B.

She has been giving a dinner to the poor children of the parish. She's been hard at work since eight o'clock this morning.

Bess.

(Looking off L.2.E.) Look at that little mite of a fellow holding on to her. They won't let her go.

Ann.

(Outside) Run back, little fellow, I'll not be long.

Mrs. V.B.

What should we do without our Ann Cruger?

Ann.

Outside) Ha, ha, ha!

(Music swells as enter Ann L.2.E. She has on a pretty white apron over her fashionable walking dress.)

Listen! Do you hear that laughing, romping babel of glee? Doesn't it make the blood rush through your veins and knock at your heart until you want to take up their baby-world in your arms and hug it?

Mrs. D.P.

Ann, anybody would think you were one of them.

Ann.

(Enthusiastically) I am. Oh, what a glorious day. On the stroke of two, the doors were thrown open. In rushed a hundred ragged little boys and girls. It would have done your heart good to have seen the awe come over them at the sight of the tables. When they were convinced it was not a dream but all real - Oh! - the grin - you could have heard it.

(All laugh)

Just then a tiny little tot, with a scream of delight, dashed head over heels for the table, climbed up in his chair and yelled, "I've beat the hull gang o' yer."

(All laugh)

Just think of those pale pinched faces, with hungry eyes and

open mouths, waiting for their struggle with the Turks. I gave the command. With a yell that would have done credit to a Comanche Tribe they tooks their places, and the attack began. Oh, Raphael! your two little fat cherubs with their angel wings are not to be compared with my lean waifs and their turkey wings.

(All laugh)

Then came the desert. I didn't know where they were going to put that, but they must have been made at the Goodyear Rubber Factory.

(Goes L. and embraces Mrs.V.B.)

Bess.

(At back) They didn't even wait to say "amen" after grace.

Alec.

(At back) Perhaps like Macbeth, amen stuck in their throats.

Ann.

(Going up into alcove L. and looking for book)

But where did I leave my story book?

Mrs.D.P.

Ann, don't you think my trip abroad has done me good? Why have you given up spending your summers in Europe?

Ann.

(Crossing R. still looking for book)

Looking at ruins becomes rather monotonous after four summers. Besides what have you there that we haven't here except London fogs and you get those from us. I'm an American and like novelty. That's why I prefer the new world. Europe after America. As I take European cheese after an American dinner.

Mrs.D.P.

Ah, you should have been with us on the Rhine, through Switzerland.

Ann.

I went up the Hudson, around the Horse-shoe Curve. I stood on the summit of Pike's Peak.

Alec.

What's the matter with Hoboken Heights?

Mrs.D.P.

Alec!

Alec.

(Suddenly remembering) I forgot the messenger!

(Exit C. precipitately)

Mrs.V.B.

You must not rouse Ann's patriotic spirit.

Ann.

But where did I leave my story book? I must run back.

(Goes out R.2.E. looking for story book.)

Mrs.D.P.

I'll go too, dear. I shouldn't be able to sit in my pew Sunday if I didn't do something for charity. I'll have a look at them.

(To Mrs.V.B.

Oh, will you come dear?

(Exit Mrs. V. B. and Mrs. D. P. L.2.E.)

Ann.

(Enter from R.2.E. with book)

Ah, here it is, Gulliver's Travels.

(Starts to go L.)

Bess.

(Coming down quickly and detaining her.)

Ann! I want to ask you something before Alec. comes back.

Ann.

Well, be quick Bess; I haven't a moment to spare.

Bess.

(Holding Ann back) Ann, how does a girl feel when she's in love?

Ann.

Really, Bess, we haven't time by four hours to discuss that subject. You shall spend the night with me, and we'll talk about it from bed time till morning. I must go, dear.

Bess.

(Holding her dress and still detaining her.)

But you go to sleep as soon as your head touches the pillow, and leave me awake to think all night.

(Drawing away from her with comic pantomine)

Is it - er - a sort - of a - of - a - a general feeling - all over you? You know.

Ann.

I do not know.

Bess.

Oh, yes you do.

Ann.

Bess --

Bess.

I know why you gave this dinner to brother John's waifs! Just beacuse - you knew - it would please - him.

Ann.

Serves me right for stopping to hear a child prattle about love. (Starting to go L.)

Bess.

Well, I know brother John's symptoms.

(Ann pauses on threshold showing interest.)

Oh, don't let me keep you.

Ann

Has brother John any -- symptoms?

Bess.

(Nodding). Um - um - want to know?

Ann.

Yes. (Coming down C.).

Bess.

Then will you keep awake to-night?

Ann.

(Sitting in chair C. by table). Yes - yes.

Bess.

(Kneeling by her) You are not anxious, are you? Well -

(Confidentially)

I heard brother John tell Angel, that he didn't know what he would do without you. That he had in his heart such a feeling for you -

(Ann, whose arm is about Bess, presses her close to her. Bess disengages herself and throws herself on floor at Ann's feet in front of her)

if you squeeze me so tight I can't tell you. Do you think you could love brother John enough to be his wife?

Ann

(Rising - confused) I - I think - that - that you can't keep a secret.

(Drawing Bess to her impulsively and kissing her)

There!

(Runs off L.2.E.)

(Re-enter Alec C.)

(S T O P  M U S I C)

Alec.

(Coming down C. with camera which he places C. then crosses to L.2.E.)

I've fixed the messenger. He's coming down to the office to-morrow during one of his errands. I'm going to give him a Chili stamp for his collection. My! my, what a racket those waifs are making. Never get 'em still long enough to take 'em.

Bess.

Going to take me too, Alec?

Alec.

I'd rather take you than any girl in New York.

Bess.

Think as much of me as you did my chum, Kitty Ives?

Alec.

More. (Coming down to her) Say, Bess.

Bess.

What is it, Alec?

Alec.

I - er - (Aside) strange! I can think of fifty ways to make a million or two, yet I can't find one way to tell her how much I love her. (Aloud) I'll tell you when I take your photograph.

Bess.

(Going L.) If you wait it'll be too dark.

Alec.

This apparatus works best in the dark. (Business of pantomine) Flash! Make your own sunlight, and there you are.

Bess.

Coney Island picture.

Alec.

I don't warrant complexion, but I guarant.e to get all your features in.

(Picking up apparatus and starting L.)

Come along, Bess, you take the plates.

Bess.

(Picking them up) My! But they're heavy!

Alec.

They'll be heavier after I get the pictures of those stuffed kids on them.

(Exeunt Bess and Alec L.?.E. laughing.)

(Enter Dick Van Buren C. with overcoat, travelling satchel etc., as though just having landed from the steamer. He is thirty-two. The terrible mental strain is visible in his care-worn face and whitening hair. Jasper follows with valise. He is followed by Creighton, a middle-aged man of the regulation brokek type.)

Dick.

(Handing overcoat to Jasper) Take them to my room --

(Exit Jasper R.I.E.)

You sent word to Paxton?

Creighton.

I telegraphed him as soon as the ship was sighted off Fire Island.

Dick.

Why didn't you cable me the moment there was a break in United Western. Couldn't you see Cruger's hand in the move?

Creighton.

It was so well guarded - so -.

Dick.

I saw it across the Atlantic. Why couldn't you see it across the street?

Damn him! (Throwing small bag on table C.) I can't stir from that office that Franklin Cruger does not take advantage of my absence. Creighton your delay has cost us half a million.

Creighton.

Better let it go, Dick, than wreck McLean & Strong, the firm stood by us.

Dick.

Let nothing go. Your tender heart would turn the Stock Exchange into a prayer meeting. There's a crisis staring us in the face and friends and foes must go to keep us on our feet. If your conscience troubles you, stay at home and let me fight it out. I'll win if I fill every alms-house from the Battery to Kings Bridge.

Creighton.

But, Dick, public opinion -

(Enter Paxton C. hurriedly.)

Dick.

Oh, Success justifies everything. It's only failure that's called to account.

Pax.

(Surprised) Mr. Van Buren! You here!

Dick.

No. (Sitting C. by table.) I'm still in Europe. You heard from me by the "Umbria" to-day. I was in Vienna, sick - on my way to the South of Italy. Have me dead, if you want to. Cruger's died three times. All I want is to keep my presence in New York unknown for three days.

Pax.

Adams & Pell were buying up United Western last night where-ever they could get their hands on it.

Creighton.

But Marsh, Fleming & Co. were selling at par.

Dick.

That's only a blind. How much are we carrying?

Pax.

Forty thousand shares -- sixty days. If the rise continues, I'm afraid sir --

Dick.

(Rising) Cruger again.

Creighton.

Cruger!

Dick.

Marsh, Fleming & Co. and Adams & Pell are both acting for him. Any day, the market may be flooded and we shall be swamped. Creighton, take a cab, drive as quickly as you can to McLean & Strong. As fast as Marsh & Fleming sell let them buy.

Creighton.

Adams & Pell are running up the price.

Dick.

Part of Cruger's scheme. Bid against them. Keep the stock out of their hands at any cost. Buy, buy, till I tell you stop.

(Creighton starts up C. gets hat.)

Paxton, go to my bed room and see if the telephone is working to the office.

Pax.

There's no one at the office to-day, sir.

Creigh.

I was going to McLean's house. It is Christmas day.

Dick.

(With an exclamation of anger)

Hang these holidays! The week is short enough as it is. Paxton get your note-book ready. (Exit Paxton R.I.E.)

Dick.

Hurry Creighton! Hurry and find McLean.

(Exit Creighton C.)

The old fool. But I made my first step with his money. When I'm through with him I'll give him a pension -- I'm shaking as though I had a chill. Not over the voyage yet, I suppose.

(Taking out flask of brandy from hand-bag and pours out brandy in cup as he continues.)

But I'm back on time to set my foot on Cruger's neck. I'll work Chicago through Campbell & Son, St. Louis, through McVeigh & Co. (Drinks) Had the "Umbria" been twenty-four hours late, Cruger would have been master of the situation. He would have upset the scheme I've had in my head for months. Son-in-law to the man that holds this continent in his hand, my name will blanch the faces of every stock exchange in the world, and then --

(Puts flask in hand-bag.)

Yes, the only way to shake this King of Wall Street from his throne and take his place is - to make Ann Cruger - my wife.

(Goes up C. and hangs hand-bag on hat-rack.)

(Bess runs on L.2.E.)

Bess.

Oh, dear! Just as Alec was ready to take them, he missed his flash light. I wonder where it is.
(Sees Dick)
Why, Dick!

Dick.

Ah, little one!

Bess.

Where in the world did you come from?
(Rushing into his arms)

Dick.

Bess, my darling.
(Taking her in his arms and kissing her fondly.)

Bess

Oh! Dick, Dick! Kiss me again.

Dick.

(Sits on Sofa R. C. taking Bess on his lap.) Tell me, dear how is mother?

Bess.

Well, but worried about you. You're better now, aren't you, Dick?

Dick.

Stronger than ever, little one.

Bess.

(Nestling close to him) Oh, I'm so glad! In your last letter from Paris, you promised me a great surprise.

Dick.

(Laughing) What was the last thing you said to me before I left?

Bess.

Oh, I said so many things - Oh! I remember!
(Rising and coming down stage a little)
I told you that Kitty Ives was having a dress made at Worth's for the Charity Ball. And if you had time, you might drop in and price one for me. (With sudden thought) Oh, you've bought it. I can see it in your eye. How did you get my measure?

Dick.

Eh? Why, I asked mother to get it from your dress-maker.

Bess.

(Throwing her arms around his neck and kissing him.)
Oh, Dick, you are so good!
(Jumping up and walking as though she had a train.)
A dress from Worth's!

Alec.

(Outside L.) Where's that flash light?

Bess.

(Starting up stage quickly) Oh, I forgot.

Dick.

(Rising and coming to her.)
See here, little one! Bess! I don't want anyone to know of m
my return except John and Mother.

Bess.

Why not?

Dick.

For reasons that you cannot understand.

Bess.

Well, after a dress from Worth's I'll tell everybody that
you're in Jerusalem.

Dick.

Simply keep these little lips (Kissing her) closed.

Bess.

That locks them.

Alec.

(Outside) Bess-s-s-s!

Bess.

Yes, Alec, I'm coming!
(Goes up stage quickly, then sees John)
Here's brother John. Get behind the curtains.
(Excitedly pushing him up into alcove L. C.)
Get behind the curtains. Quick! When I say "booh" come out.
(Dick laughingly submits.)

(Warningly, with uplifted finger)
Mind now, don't stir till I say "booh".
(Enter John Van Buren R.3.E. He is thirty-five years of age. No grey in his hair. His manner easy and natural. His dress that of the fashionable clergymnn of to-day.)
(Inpulsively) Brother John! Dick's behind the curtain!

John.
(Laughingly) None of your tricks. Why Dick's in Paris.

Bess.
No-o-o-o! Behind the curtain.
(Gesticulating wildly towards curtains.)

John.
Who?

Bess.
Dick.

John.
Our Dick?

Bess.
Yes. I put him there to surprise you. He wasn't to come out until I - Oh - I forgot. Booh!

Dick.
(Throwing curtains aside) Hello, John.
(Dick comes down and grasps John's hand warmly.)
(Bess darts up stage and gets flash light - comes down and one arm around the neck of each - kisses John - and then kisses Dick twice.)

John.
Why, Dick, Dick old fellow, I'm so glad.

Alec.
(Outside) Hurry up, Bess. These waifs can't smile like this all night. They'll go into hysterics.

Bess.
(Darting under their clasped hands and going L.)
I'm coming, Alec. I'm coming. (Stops) Oh, Dick, may I tell Angel you are here?

Dick.
Yes.

Bess.

Oh, I'm so happy. A dress from Worth's.

(Bess runs off with flash light L.2.E.)

John.

Dick, why didn't you cable us?

Dick.

I wanted to take Cruger unawares. I didn't dare trust a message even to the wires.

John.

The doctor ordered absolute rest. You should have obeyed him.

Dick.

And let Cruger down me--but there, old fellow! Aren't you glad to see me?

John.

Glad? Why, ever since the day I saw your haggard face looking at me from the ship, as she moved out of the dock, I've looked forward to your return with an anxiety - well, that you ought to understand, knowing what we have been to each other.

Dick.

John, old fellow, you're a brick. But what was I to do? For months I have been maturing a plan --

John.

(Sadly) Always plans!

Dick.

This one, John will place me at the top.

(M U S I C)

(His arm around John's neck)

Old fellow, you're not practical enough.

John.

It is what I see in this practical world of yours that makes me fear for you.

Dick.

I'm all right.

(M U S I C +

John.

Not long ago I stood by the bed of a dying man, whose name in the business world had been a synonym of honor. This money fever seized him. More and more eager he became in his greed for wealth; until he ended - a fugitive from home, body and soul burnt out by this delirium of speculation. As I listened at the last to his words, a chill came over me, Dick, I was thinking of you.

Dick.

No, no, I love you all too much to let that be my end.

John.

He had loved ones too.

(During the above Dick has been nervously turning the leaves of the album.)

Yet, I never heard a sadder story than that of --

Dick.

(Seeing picture in album - starting) Phyllis Lee!

John.

You know her?

Dick.

(Recovering) No.

John

(Crossing to R. of Dick behind him)
You saw the name on the picture -

Dick.

Yes.

John.

Strange coincidence! It was of her father that I was speaking

Dick.

How came her picture in the album?

John.

(Standing beside Dick at the table)
Because - Dick - the pity that I first felt for her became after a time --

Dick.

(Reels, about to fall). Does he love her?

John.

(Quickly turns and catches him in his arms) Dick!

(S T O P   M U S I C)

You see you should not have returned so soon. You are in no fit condition for business.

(Enter Mrs. V. B. L.2.E.)

(Apart to Dick) Here's mother!

Mrs.V.B.

(Embracing Dick) My boy! my boy! I'm so glad you're home again.

Dick.

Mother, dear. (With his arm around her) Remember, John, not a word of my presence here.

John.

His thoughts on Wall Street even in his mother's arms.

(John, with a sigh, turns up stage and exits R.2.E.)

Mrs.V.B.

It's at a time like this that I wish I were not blind. I want to see my boy. Come, come, tell me all about yourself.

Dick.

Presently, mother, presently. Tell me first about that picture in the album --

Mrs. V.B.

Picture?

Dick.

A Miss Lee.

( M U S I C )

Mrs. V.B.

Oh! John's protege. Has he been speaking to you about her.

Dick.

Yes.

Mrs.V.B

He's very much interested in her. My! I forgot to let him know.

Dick.

Has he heard from her recently?

Mrs. V.B.

Why, you seem as much interested as John. I have invited her to come here to us for a while.

(Phyllis comes slowly on R. R. E. she does not see the others.)

Dick.

(Aside) Coming here? (Aloud) When do you expect her?

Mrs.V.B.

Why, she is --

(At this moment Phyllis who has come on sees Dick and with a start, stops. Dick at the same instant sees her, and stands transfixed with surprise. She is about to speak his name and rush to him when he checks her. This mutual recognition, unknown to the blind mother is marked.)

(With a pleasant smile) If I am not mistaken, she is here now. Phyllis.

Phyllis.

(Coming down) Mrs. Van Buren!

Mrs.V.B.

I want to introduce you to my boy. Dick, this is Phyllis Lee.

(They do not bow or give any show of greeting to deceive the mother. As she is blind, the strength of this situation is in their remaining immovable.)

In the joy of my boy's unexpected return, I forgot to tell John of your arrival. I'll let him know. Dick, make Miss Lee realize that she is at home.

(Exit R.2.E.)

Phyllis.

(Rushing to him and clasping her arms tight around his neck.)

Dick! Dick!

Dick.

(Quietly removing her arms) Be careful Phyllis.

Phyllis.

It's so long since I've seen you.

Dick.

Yes, yes, I know, dear - but --

Phyllis

Aren't you glad to see me?

Dick.

Why, of course I am.

Phyllis.

When father died, and your brother said I must come here, I felt like going down on my knees and telling him of our love. Nothing but my promise to you kept me silent. Dick, don't say I did wrong to come - Don't.

Dick.

(Aside) Why should I let a promise to a woman stand between me and success?

Phyllis.

Oh, Dick, don't let me live here a lie. They're all so good to me. Oh! when am I to take my place among them?

John.

(Outside R.) Very well, mother, I'll send her to you.

(Dick crosses R.)

(Enter John R.2.E.)

(Advancing with outstretched hands) Welcome to the Rectory.

Phyllis.

Mr. Van Buren, you don't know how much those words mean to me.

(Turns away towards window.)

John.

(Aside to Dick) Now that you have seen her, doesn't her sad face appeal to you? (John turns to Phyllis)

Dick.

(Aside) If I could only tear this love out of my heart. I will!

(Exit R.I.E.)

John.

My mother wants you to go to the study. And while you are talking to her I'm going to consult Ann Cruger about you. She is the dearest friend I have in the world - and I want you to know her.

Phyllis.

(Affected) You are so kind to me, Mr. Van Buren, that I -

John.

It is my privilege. (Leading her to R.2.E.) Come, mother is waiting for you. As the light of day never comes to her eyes, Heaven has put into her heart a sunlight, brightening the lives of all that look upon her face. Go to her - there

must be no more sad days. In this house you will find only happiness.

(Exit Phyllis R.2.E.)

(Enter Ann L.2.E.)

Ann.

(Places apron, which she takes off, and book, on stand in alcove)

Well!

John.

Hello, Ann!

Ann.

I wondered if you had forgotten all about us.

John.

I was detained upon an urgent call. I'm so sorry not to have seen the children at their dinner.

Ann.

(Coming down) I have read "Gulliver's Travels" until I'm exhausted. They sent me to find out if you had come.

John.

I am sure they don't need any one else while they have you.

Ann.

'Tis such a pleasure to me. I would have been alone to-day if I had stayed at home. Papa of course can't go to business so he is spending the day with his brokers. They dine together.

John.

Well, but don't you look upon this as your home?

Ann.

It has always seemed so, John -

John.

You make us all as happy here as Christmastide as you have made those children. It wouldn't seem like Christmas if you were not here to share it with us.

Ann.

And it wouldn't be Christmas to me if I had to spend it anywhere else.

John.

(Starting to go up L. with her.)

Come then - I don't want to deprive the children too long of their good fairy.

Judge.

(Outside R.) Don't you try to bolt from me, sir. Hold onto him, Jasper. Hold onto him! Where are the pôlice. Somebody! Anybody!

(Judge enters from R.3.E. He is about 55, hale, vigorous a trifle quaint in attire and old fashioned in his methods.)

Ann! I'm glad to find you.

(Coming down. Putting hat on stand R. and throwing overcoat on back of sofa)

Hello John. "Tantaene animus caelestibus irae."

Ann.

Why are you storming away in Latin?

Judge.

It's safer in a clergyman's presence. Besides, my English would disgrace me. In my judicial capacity I have sentenced everything from a boot-black to a blackmailer, from a wife-beater to a lady-killer. But never has there appeared before me, such a corpuscle of humanity as I have just deposited in the hall.

Ann.

Goodness!

Judge.

I came upon him as he was breaking into the parish buildings.

Ann.

Through one of the windows?

Judge.

No, squeezing himself through the gratings.

Ann.

How could he do it?

Judge.

Do it? He looked as if he could eat an iron bar.

(Going up)

Ann.

Heavens!

Judge.

Come in you floatsem, jetsam, ligan. What, you won't?

(Starting out)

John.

Shall I help you Judge?

Judge.

No - Alone I captured him, single handed I'll bring him here.

(Goes off R.3.E.)

Ann.

(Going to extreme L.) Well, I'm afraid to stay.

Judge.

(Outside) Let him go, Jasper. The strong right hand of the law is upon him.

(Judge re-appears dragging on Cain, a mite of a boy, ragged, coatless, shoeless, his shirt peeping through a rent in his trousers. His face is pale and pinched. The Judge holds him at arm's length.)

There! What do you say to that?

Ann.

That you were right - you dear old god-father to bring him here.

John.

And I thought it was some desperate criminal.

Judge.

Criminal? Isn't that criminal enough? Criminal negligence. We send missionaries to Borioboolagha with a thing like that on our doorstep. Come here!

(Placing him on chair)

Get up here and let's have a look at you.

(Cain turns his back to the audience showing rent)

Turn around the other way, sir.

(Cain turns around facing the audience)

Ann.

Poor little fellow!

(Taking both his hands in hers)

Why, how cold your hands are!

John.

And he looks so hungry.

Ann.

Hungry! (Calls) Sophie!

Judge.

Ann, have you got a pin?

Ann.

(Giving pin) Yes, here, what do you want it for?

Judge.

Your sex is altogether too inquisitive.

(Sophie appears at L.2.E.)

You tell Sophie what you want with her.

(Ann meets Sophie up stage and gives directions. Judge meanwhile quickly stuffs shirt in trousers and pins the rents.)

There! I have expelled the winter's flaw. Now then, sit down.

(Cain sits then springs up with a cry of pain.)

Judge and Ann.

What's the matter?

(Exit Sophie L.2.E.)

Cain.

Pin.

Ann.

Oh, Judge!

Judge.

Ann, if you had given me a safety pin that wouldn't have happened.

Ann.

Why, what is this?

(Taking cigarettes out of Cain's pocket)

Judge.

Cigarettes.

Cain.

Gi' me 'um.

(Snatching them from Ann and putting one in mouth)

Judge?

(Snatching them from Cain) Can I get you a light. They would kill a goat. Avenue A. Perfectos.

(Throws them on floor R.)

Ann.

What's your name?

Cain.

Cain.

Judge.

Eh?

Cain.

Cain.

Judge.

Cain? Cain, what?

Cain.

Cain nothin'. Just plain Cain.

Judge.

Where did you get that name?

Cain.

A kind lady called me that 'cause she said I was a wanderer on the face o' the earth.

Judge.

What is your father's name?

Cain.

Burglin' Billy.

Judge.

Ann, you ask him his mother's name; I'm afraid.

Ann.

(Tenderly) But your mother, lityle boy. She has a name?

Cain.

Never had no mother.

Judge.

Oh! Poor little - um! Where is your father?

Cain.

In Jail.

Ann.

Have you any brothers or sisters?

(Cain nods head)

Where are they?

Cain.

In jail.

Judge.

Where do you expect to go?

Cain.

(With a wry face) Jail.

Judge.

John, the law gives him up. I hand him over to the church.

John.

And the church hands him over to the care of woman. Here, Ann, you take him.

Judge.

Yes, Ann can raise Cain if she likes. (Aside) I never saw a woman who couldn't.

Ann.

I told Sophie to go and get some turkey - pudding - ice-cream - oranges --

(She watches the effect of each word)

Cain.

(A grin breaking over his face as he rubs his stomach)

Yum!

Ann.

I have sent for enough to make even a strong man tremble.

Judge.

Why, a strong man is nothing to a small boy like that.

Ann.

But first I must take you up stairs and wash your face. Look at that! Come along little boy.

(Exit with Cain upstairs R.3.E.)

Judge.

Well, if Ann puts Cain into the bath-tub there'll be nothing left of him. Mrs. De Peyster is here, Jasper told me so. I gave him a dollar. It was worth it. John, I was afraid I wouldn't be in time to see Ann with the children. A coal cart broke down in front of my car and blockaded the whole road.

John.

Why didn't you take the elevated?

Judge.

No, I never do that on principle. We hurry enough through life now-a-days without rushing upstairs to ride in the air. I tried it once. John, when we went around that hundred and tenth Street curve, I could have sworn I heard harps. There is only one car line in the city that travels with a dignified and stately ease. That's the Belt Line. That takes me back forty years to the time when your father and I used to run with the machine, along with Harry Howard, and Zophar Mills and the rest of the boys. Ah, John times have changed, times have changed. Why, it was only yesterday in Court, young Livingston, a fledgling just beginning to toddle with the aid of Blackstone under one arm, and Chitty on Pleading, under the other, had the impertinence to teach me law. When I told him that I had sat on the bench for thirty years, what do you think he replied?

John.

Why, what?

Judge.

"Get up and give the bench a rest."

(John laughs heartily.)

I gave him a night's rest - for contempt of Court.

John.

Never mind, Judge, there is one person who believes in you thoroughly.

Judge.

Oh, your dear mother!

John.

No - I - I alluded to Mrs. De Peyster.

Judge.

Charming woman! Delightful woman! I called upon her to-day to pay my respects, but she was out.

John.

She is here.

Judge.

You don't tell me.

John.

Oh, yes, yes. (Aside.) As if he didn't know. I was just on my way to see the children in the Parish buildings where she is now.

Judge.

John, I don't mind telling you. Do you know she came very near being Mrs. Peter Gurney Knox.

John.

Indeed! What prevented?

Judge.

Oh, nothing. Only De Peyster was too quick for me. However he was one of your fast livers, and got through early - Now, John --

(Taking his arm confidentially)

You are my clergyman, and it's no more than right that you should know of the state of my feelings towards one of your clients - (Correcting himself) I mean parishioners -

John.

You don't mean to tell me that you love her still.

Judge.

That's it, John, a still love. I'm getting along in years, you know. Face a little furrowed. But John, there are no wrinkles on my heart. Ha, ha, ha - I saw her. Last night at the theatre and she looked so radiant that I determined to bring this matter to an issue at once, and I want to borrow this room to do it in.

John.

With pleasure. I'll send her to you.

Judge.

If you will be so kind.

John.

(Going L.) Certainly - certainly. Fortune favors the brave. She is coming this way.

Judge.

(Very nervously) Well, John, on second thought I'll just step inside and then come in and take her accidentally - you know.

John.

Oh, you'll come in accidentally.

(Goes out R.3.E. forgetting hat and overcoat. Enter Mrs. D. P. - L.2.E. limping.)

Mrs.D.P.
Mr. Van Buren, may I trouble you for your arm? I'm afraid I've sprained my ankle.

John.
(Assisting her down steps). I trust not.

Mrs.D.P.
Dear! I can hardly stand.

John.
(Putting her in chair C. table).
Sit here.
(Enter Judge hurriedly from R.3.E.)

Judge.
(Aside). Oh! I thought the coast was clear. I'm not ready for a clergyman yet.
(Exit precipitately.)

Mrs.D.P.
Will you kindly ask Alec to come to me?

John.
Certainly - certainly.
(X'ing to L.2.E. looks off C.)
She is now at his mercy.
(Exit L.2.E.)

Mrs.D.P.
Dear, dear! I do hope this will pass off before Judge Knox arrives. There is no misunderstanding that letter. "When next we meet prepare to be astounded." Yes, he means to propose.
(Sees Judge's hat and crosses to it.)
Eh? Why - that looks like his hat. It is "Knox" - dear, dear, dear, he must be here. I should be mortified to be obliged to limp during a declaration of love.
(Starting to go R.)
Before he comes I'll apply some arnica.
(Judge enters as before and comes down C.)

Judge.
Ah, my esteemed friend.

Mrs.D.P.
(Aside) Too late.
(Stands with difficulty, endeavoring to conceal from Judge that she is in pain.)

Judge.

(Shaking hands with her.) This is indeed an unexpected delight.

Mrs.D.P.

How do you do, Judge, how do you do?

Judge.

Our first meeting since your return. I should have arrived sooner if I had known you were here.

Mrs.D.P.

Oh, come, come, Judge. You haven't just arrived.

Judge.

(Protesting.) Oh, but -

Mrs.D.P.

Isn't this your hat?

Judge.

(Taking hat from her - aside.) "Where did you get that hat!" I suppose I shall find my brains in the lining.
(Aloud) Well, to tell the truth, I was here, and when I heard you coming --

Mrs. D.P.

You ran away.

Judge.

The evidence of this witness - is so conclusive that any attempt at prevarication would only render myself liable - (Bowing) to the contempt of the court.
(Places hat on table C.).

Mrs.D.P.

(Aside) I feel my ankle swelling.

Judge.

I never saw you looking better.

Mrs.D.P.

Thank you, Judge!

Judge.

The bloom of the peach is on your cheek, the sparkle of the diamond in your eye. The air of contented ease with which you stand there -
(Mrs.D.P. looks up showing pain)

is only equalled when you walk by that poetry of motion that always charms me.

Mrs.D.P.

Thanks, Judge! (Aside) I would rather die than move an inch. (Aloud) Oh, Judge, you spoil me.

Judge.

Did you receive a letter from me?

Mrs.D.P.

A letter? Oh, yes.

Judge.

I will now explain why I wrote it.
(Turns to get a chair up R.)

Mrs.D.P.

(Aside) He is going to - oo!
(Sits quickly)

Judge.

(Turning quickly) You remarked?

Mrs.D.P.

Nothing, Judge, nothing. (Aside) Oh, dear, dear! To be so afflicted at such a moment.

Judge.

(Bringing down chair and sitting L. of Mrs.D.P.)
I wish to warn you against a certain man, whose name I will not mention. He has designs upon you.

Mrs.D.P.

(In alarm) On me, Judge?

Judge.

Don't be alarmed. As your legal adviser I shall protect you. Unfortunately I am his legal adviser also, and must look after his interests. He loves you; loved you long before your De Peyster experience.

Mrs.D.P.

(Heaving a sigh) Oh, Judge!

Judge.

But he has none of those soft ways that ladies admire.

Mrs.D.P.

And yet, you plead his cause.

Judge.

As his legal adviser.

Mrs.D.P.

(Aside) This shoe is killing me.

Judge.

He is a bad tempered, selfish, inconsiderate man, a man well calculated to render any woman's life unendurable. From infancy I have been his most intimate friend. And I warn you against him.

Mrs.D.P.

And his name, Judge?

Judge.

Peter Gurney Knox.

Mrs.D.P.

Oh, Judge, you give yourself such a character?

Judge.

As your legal adviser.

Mrs.D.P.

(Aside - with pain) Oh!

Judge.

(Rising) It is for you to give the decision. I have summed up for both clients. I leave the matter in the hands of the court.

Mrs.D.P.

(Aside) I cannot endure this another moment.

Judge.

You hesitate.

Mrs.D.P.

Oh, Judge!

Judge.

I warn you, if you decide against my client, Knox, we will appeal the case.

Mrs.D.P.

Oh, Judge, I am suffering such intense pain!

Judge.

(Sitting by her side on sofa) On my account?

Judge.

(Nearer) In your heart?

Mrs.D.P.

No, in my foot. An accident.

Judge.

Accident?

Mrs.D.P.

But oblige me by dismissing it from your mind.

Judge.

(Very close) Then I may hope. Speak, Camilla!
(Enter Alec L.2.E.)

Alec.

Want me, auntie?

Mrs.D.P.

(Aside) Thank Heaven!

Judge.

(Rising - aside) To interrupt proceedings at such a juncture!

Alec.

Judge, you were all wrong about that Livingston affair.

Judge.

(Putting chair up R.) I hope sir, I taught him proper decorum in the presence of the court.

Alec.

You broke up our party at the Casino. 'Twas Bob's night to put up for the supper, too. The idea of committing a fellow for a little thing like that.

Judge.

The next time he has a case before me, he'll give the bench a rest.

Alec.

(Aside) I'll get square with the Judge yet.

Mrs.D.P.

(Apart to Alec) Alec! Alec! Open the door, open the door. I've sprained my ankle. I don't want the Judge to see me leave the room.

(Mrs. De Peyster quickly goes L. limping. Alec, at that moment opens the folding doors. Before she reaches the doors, with a cry of pain, she sinks into a large arm chair. Alec wheels the chair out of the room, and quickly closing the folding doors stands before them, facing the Judge, who has turned in time to see Mrs. De Peyster disappear. For a moment they look at each other.)

Judge.

Most remarkable manner of leaving a room.

Alec.

Yes, a little hurried.

Judge.

Nothing serious, I hope. She spoke of her foot.

Alec.

Yes, her foot is off.

Judge.

Her foot is off?

Alec.

(Aside) I wonder if he knows she has a sprained ankle. (Aloud) Of course, Judge, you know what's the matter?

Judge.

She spoke of an accident.

Alec.

She didn't tell you what it was?

Judge.

No.

Alec.

Oh, no, of course not. She couldn't.

Judge.

Why not?

Alec.

(Aside) Oh! This is good. I can't lose it. (Aloud) I say Judge, to-day the first time you've seen Auntie since she returned from Paris?

Judge.

Yes!

Alec.

(Confidentially) Did you notice a slight impediment in her gait? (Pantomine) That sort of thing!

Judge.

No, you mention it, she didn't move.

Alec.

Yes, Auntie is terribly sensitive about it.

Judge.

(Impatiently) About what, sir? About what?

Alec.

I can't confide this, except under certain circumstances. Now Judge, man to man, is there anything between you and Auntie?

Judge.

Why yes, I have this day invited your esteemed Auntie to become Mrs. Knox.

Alec.

Then you ought to know. The accident she referred to happened in Paris, and the result of it was --

Judge.

Was what sir? Was what?

Alec.

Well - (Whispers in Judge's ear)

Judge.

(Aghast, sinking into chair C. by table.)

Cork!!

Alec.

On the Q. T., Judge.

(Drawing his quickly across his leg just above his ankle)

To there..

Judge.

To where?

Alec.

(Drawing his hand across leg just below knee)

To there!

Judge.

(With a groan of despair buries his head in hands on table)

Oh!

Alec.

I say, Judge, Auntie's a good business investment. When she becomes Mrs. Knox, if you ever get into trouble, she'll keep you afloat.

(Exit L.C.E.)

Judge.

(Half dazed) I must withdraw. It must be done honorably, but I must withdraw. That cork member stands between us. And I am invited to meet her at dinner this evening!

(Taking his coat and hat.)

I will ask Mrs. Van Buren, to place me as far away from her as possible. If they serve me with the second joint of the turkey, and she looks at me, I shall betray myself at once. Love! Sweet misery! Only to think of it! Some of her here, and some of her gone to join De Peyster.

(Exit R.1.E.)

(Enter Bess L.2.E.)

(W A R M   M U S I C)

Bess.

Come along, Mr. Betts.

(Goes up and gets matches from mantel.)

(Phyllis enters R.2.E.)

Phyllis.

(Aside) In his home! my home by right - and Dick was so cold, so strange - to me. Not even glad to see me! Oh, if I have no place here what will become of me!

Bess.

(Speaking off L/2.E.)

Come along.

(Betts enters with Lamp which he places on table C.).

Thank you.

Bess.

(Seeing Phyllis) Why you've come down stairs. (To Phyllis)

street, next to the chapel, and walk in.

Betts.

It's a way Mr. Van Buren has of making things easy for those that need him.

Phyllis.

Let me light the lamp to-night.

Bess.

(Striking match) Why, of course! It will celebrate your coming here.

(Hands match to Phyllis who lights lamp.)

Will you put the lamp in the window, Mr. Betts?

(S T O P   M U S I C)

Betts.

Why, of course I will.

(Taking up the lamp and singing.)

"There's a light in the window for thee." &c.

(As he exits R.2.E.)

Bess.

I want to introduce Alec to Miss Lee. I've told him all about you. He's just dying to take your photograph.

(Exeunt Bess and Phyllis L.2.E. The firelight in the alcove now floods the room. As the scene progresses the sunset fades away into twilight. Ann Cruger comes down the stairs R.3.E. with Cain, whose face is washed and hair combed. He has in his hand a piece of pie, of which he occasionally takes a bite.)

Ann.

Well, come along little fellow, did you have enough to eat?

Cain.

I've etten so much, mum, I'm tired. (Takes a bite of pie.)

Ann.

You hate to waste that pie, don't you?

(Jasper goes on L.2.E. lights the three electric lamps in alcove - goes over and lights lamp in entry-way up C. Lights piano lamp, then electric lamp above platform R.3.E. and exits R.3.E.)

Cain.

I'm loadin' up now, for to-morrow.

Ann.

You just take care of to-day. I'll take care of to-morrow.

Cain.

(Looking up into her face.)
You're awful good to a little sun-of-a-gun-

Ann.

Poor little fellow! Why you are so sleepy you can hardly keep your eyes open.

(Taking him up to rocking chair in alcove and arranging him comfortably.)

You just come here, little fellow - I'll fix you comfortably. Come here, dear! There now. Put your head on that nice soft cushion, dear. There! Isn't that comfortable?

(Cain is almost asleep.)

Did you say it was comfortable? (Aside) Poor little fellow! Why, I believe he's asleep already. And to think that he's only one of thousands in this great city.

(Sophie enters L.3.E. with armful of toys.)

Sh!

(Ann takes toys from Sophie, who then crosses R. and exits R.2.E. - Ann proceeds to fill Cain's lap with the toys, humming softly Sullivan's "Lullaby" - then pauses.)

Oh, I can't keep Bess' words out of my mind. "I heard brother John tell Angel that he didn't know what he would do without you"---

(Pauses - then continues humming the Lullaby and arranging toys as before.)

Oh, how my heart beats! Alone I may speak the words, "John, I love you."

(Continues humming the "Lullaby" and arranging the toys)

There!

(Coming down R. C. as John enters L.2.E.)

Now, when he wakes up he'll think---

John.

(Going to Cain and placing his hand lightly on his head)
That an angel has been here.

Ann.

(Turning - softly) Sh!

Cain.

(Muttering in his sleep.)
Awful -- good -- to -- a little son-of-a-gun.

John.

(Coming down L. C.)
Alec is taking their pictures - individually and in groups, on their feet and on their heads.

Ann.

Yes, I know; they are having a glorious time.

John.

And it's all owing to you. Ann, there is something I want to say to you. I must tell you to-night-- now, while we are alone.

Ann.

Is it so very important?

John.

My happiness depends upon it.

Ann.

(Aside) My heart will betray me.

(Enter Sophie R.1/E. carrying a salver on which is a small teapot, sugar-dish, two cups and saucers; and plate and biscuit. She places it on table, and taking box of matches which Bess has left on table, exits L.2.E. Ann crosses R.)

(Aside) I said I wanted a cup of tea, but I don't. Thank you Sophie. (Nervously) John, won't you have a sip of cake, and a bite of tea-- no, no, I mean-- a bite of tea, and a sip of cake -- well here are cakes and tea.

John.

Why, Ann you seem confused.

Ann.

Well - no, I can't see to talk very well in the twilight.

John.

I'll turn on the light.

Ann.

(Quickly) Oh, no-- no-- not on my account. Won't you have a cup of tea?

John.

(Bringing chair from R. up stage to table C.)

Thank you, no-- while you take yours, I'll speak to you.

Ann.

Well, I hope I won't disturb you; I'm as hungry as a bear.

John.

(Sitting at table so as not to face Ann; he must be unconscious of her embarrassment.)

Ann, you and I have been near to each other all our lives.

(Business of Ann putting several lumps of sugar in cup.)

As children we were playmates-- read together out of the same books-- and now that we are man and woman it seems natural for you to share all my confidences. You have been such a help to me in my work, I don't know what I could do without you.

(Ann unconsciously pours tea into sugar bowl.)

You have made everybody happy here to-day. The heart that has room for so many must have room for one more.

(Looking at her)

But, you are not eating and you said you were hungry.

Ann.

Oh, yes, yes, I am. Go on, John, I am listening.

John.

I love someone whose heart I do not know. The fear of disturbing her by making known my feelings, the dread of interfering with the friendship that now exists between us has kept me silent.

Ann.

Have you ever shown her that you care for her?

John.

She may have guessed it.

Ann.

Her decernment must be better than mine; for this is the first time I ever suspected that you were in love.

John.

What am I to do?

Ann.

Much depends upon the woman. I suppose you're aware-- you haven't told me who she is.

John.

She is an angel.

Ann.

(Who has the cup raised to her lips without drinking.)

Is she a New York angel?

John.

I met her first in Florida.

Ann.

(Slowly lowering the cup from her lips, without drinking)

Florida!

(W A R N  C H I M E S )

John.

I was sent for to minister to the last hours of her father. I looked across that bed of sickness, and saw her kneeling on the other side. She turned her eyes to me; I saw in them a look that told of suffering, a mute appeal that made me pity her. And as I looked -- I loved.

Ann.

(Half-dazed, but with a superhuman effort to control herself.)

Loved?

(At this moment the chimes are heard for evening service, they continue till end of act.)

John.

Something in her face as it looked into mine, connected her with my life. (Rises.)

Ann.

You are speaking of Phyllis Lee?

John.

Yes.

Ann.

Aside-- with a half moan.) Oh--

(C H I M E S)

(W A R N  M U S I C)

(W A R N  C U R T A I N)

John.

Now, do you understand why I ask you to find room in your heart for one more?

Ann.

(Slowly raising her eyes to his.)

Yes, John!

John.

I must go now to be ready for evening service. When you know her well, tell me what to do.

(Exit R.2.E.)

Ann.

He-- loves-- Phyllis-- Lee. Phyllis Lee! --

(Cain, who is asleep up in alcove makes a movement which causes the toys to fall to the floor. Ann's attention is attracted to him.)

Ah-- little fellow. I thought you were very wretched, but there are lots of people in this world, who have plenty to eat and plenty to wear, (Rising) and yet are a thousand times more wretched than you.-- a thousand times more wretched than you.

(R I N G  M U S I C)

(R I N G  C U R T A I N)

(Throws herself on steps leading up into alcove, at Cain's feet, sobbing aloud. Cain wakes up and regards her wonderingly as curtain descends.)

-%- C U R T A I N -%-

---oOo---

# THE CHARITY BALL.

## ACT II.

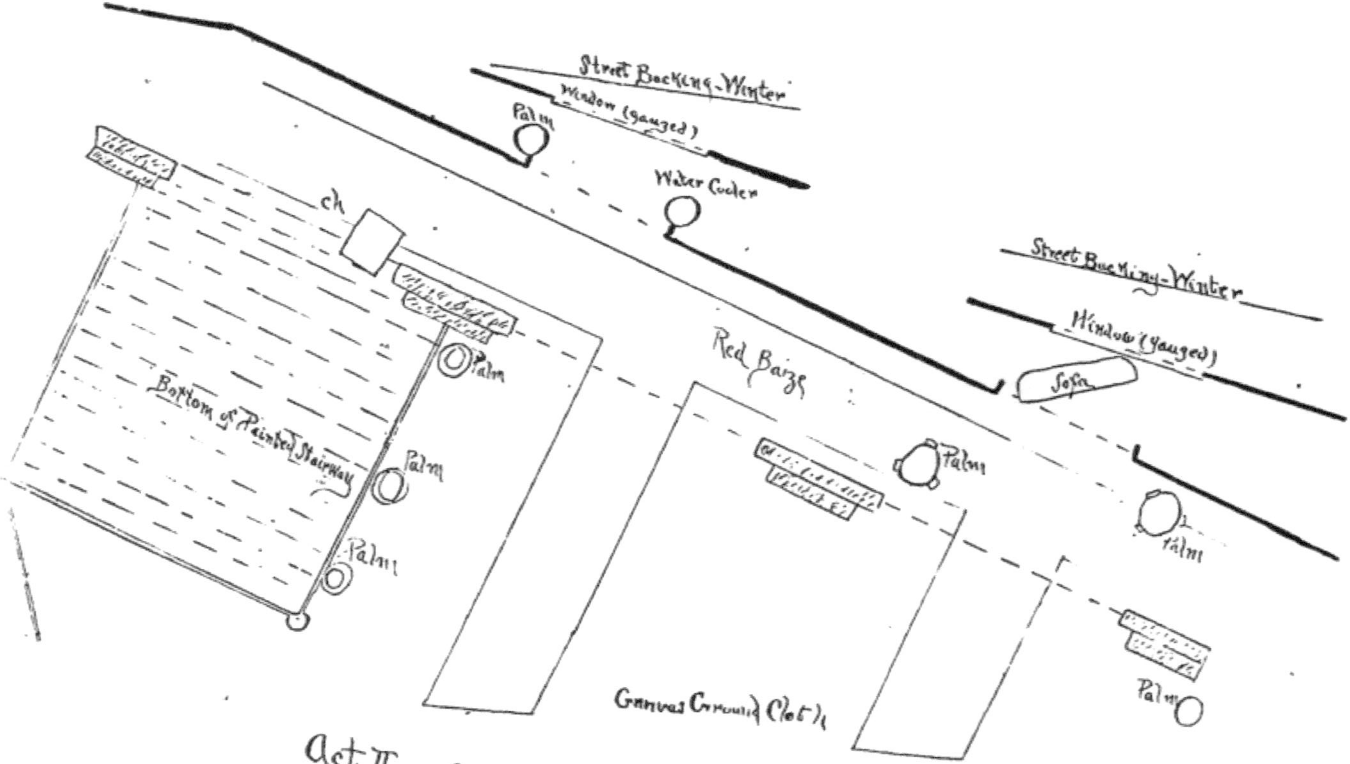


Act II Corridor at Metropolitan Opera House, N Y

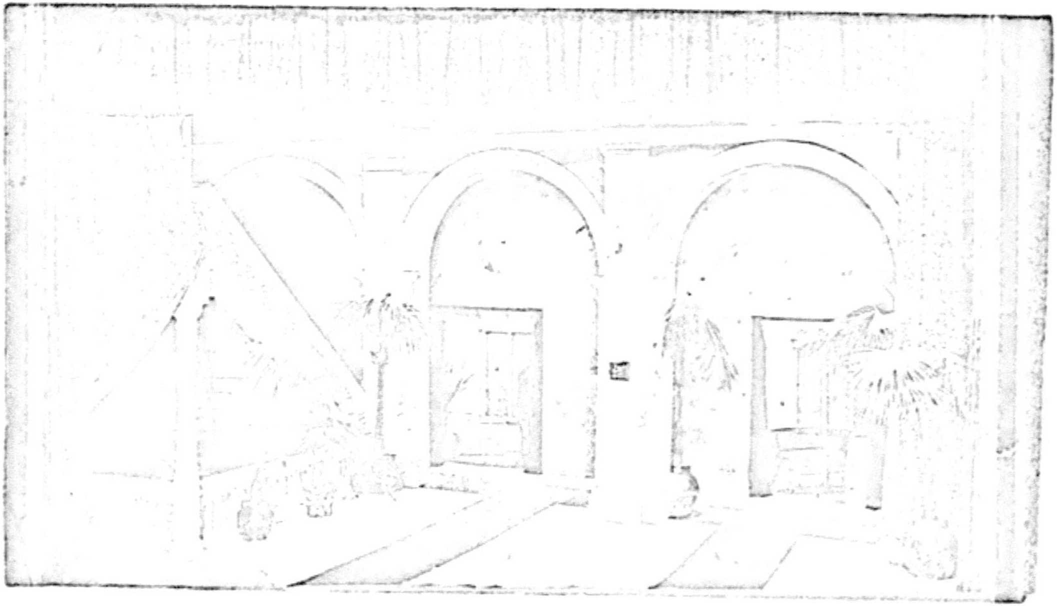

Act 2nd

## PROPERTY PLOT --- A C T I I.

---oOo---

Ground Cloth and Red Baize as shown in Diagram.

Palms as indicated.

Water-cooler in door-way up R. C.

Small Settee or Sofa up L. C.

Chair up R. C. (Back of False Stairway.)

## SIDE PROPERTIES --- A C T II.

--0-0-0--

Tray, Two Silver Cups, and Water Pitcher, (to be dropped) and Napkin, for Jasper.

25 cent silver piece and White silk handkerchief for Alec.

"Charity Ball" badge for Judge Knox.

Cigar-Case -- two Cigars -- for Cruger.

Three or four "Charity Ball" Dance cards.

--:0:--

## L I G H T S ------------ A C T II.

As indicated in Diagram. All lights up full. House lights on 3/4 throughout Act.

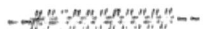

--#"#"#"#"#"--

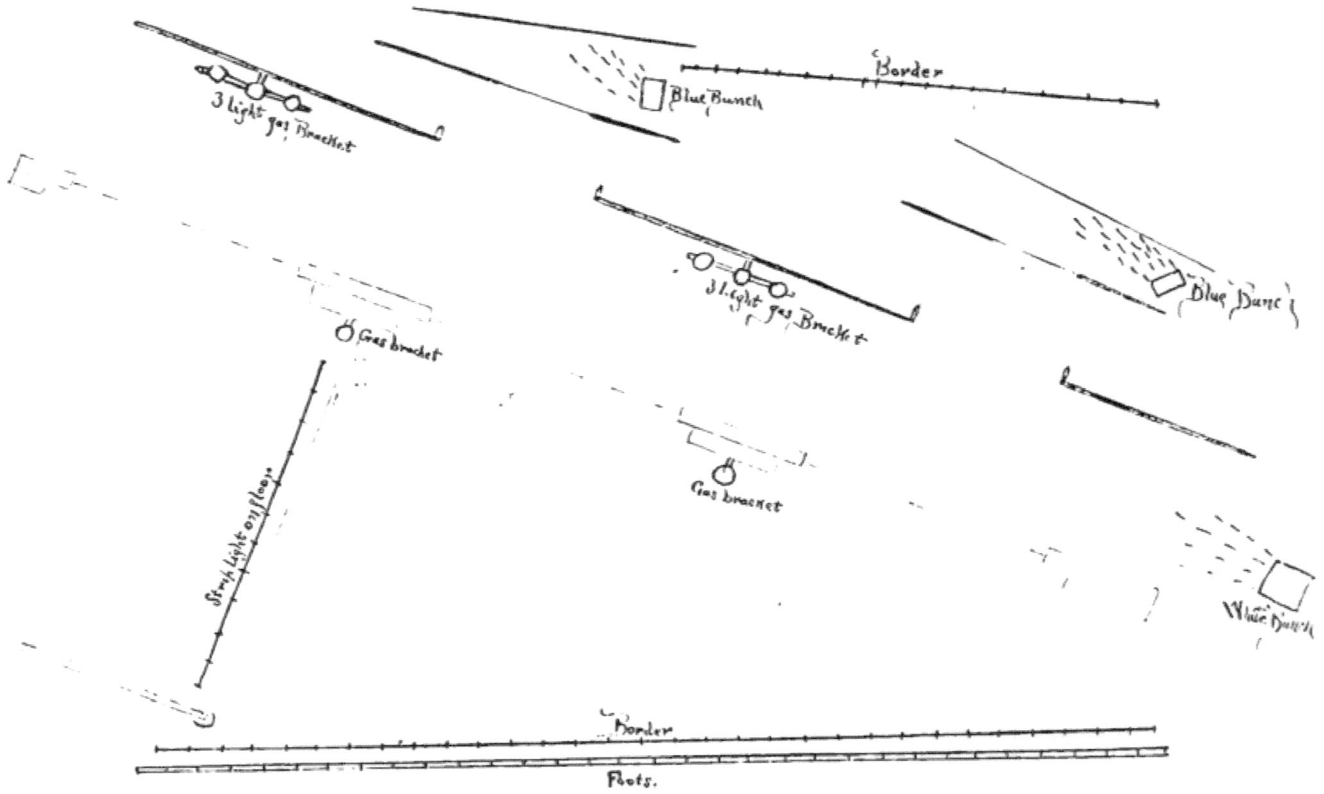
Border
3 light gas Bracket
Blue Bunch
Blue Bunch
3 light gas Bracket
Gas bracket
Gas bracket
Strip light on floor
White Bunch
Border
Foots.

# THE CHARITY BALL.

## ACT II.

(MUSIC)

SCENE:- Ante-room of Corridor at the Metropolitan Opera House, New York, brilliantly lighted and decorated with rare plants. For arrangement of scene, see diagram. Through the windows is seen the snow covered exterior-- a bleak winter's night. No snow falling. Light effects, seen through windows.
The night of the Charity Ball-- two weeks later.
Waltz heard off in ball-room.

DISCOVERED:- Jasper entering from R. U. E. with silver water pitcher, two silver goblets and a napkin on a small salver. He X'es and is about to exit L. when Alec enters L. U. E. running against him, upsetting the (supposed) water on the threshold.

Alec.

I beg your pardon. (Coming R.) That's what I've been doing all night; upsetting things. I'm upset myself.

(Crossing to Jasper L. and handing him coin.)

(To Jasper) Here! Remove the flood!

(Jasper picks up pitcher and goblets and sops up the (supposed) water with napkin and exits L.I.E.)

When I started Judge Knox on that cork joke, I never thought it would turn out so serious. Oh! I'm in an awful fix.

(Looking at card)

Next dance, polka, Bess. Next quadrille, Bess. Next schottische, Bess. I've got all the shares in that girl, anyhow. No margin for any other fellow to-night.

Bess.

(Entering L.U.E.)
Alec, what did you run away for?
(About to come into the room.)

Alec.

I didn't want to meet Judge Knox. Be careful Bess.

Bess.

Why, what's the matter?

Alec.

You're in a pool.

Bess.

(Drawing back) Oh! Gracious!

Alec.

And you've slippers on with paper soles.
(As if about to take off his coat.)
I can't do as Sir Walter Raleigh did with his Queen Bess, nineteenth century etiquette will not permit. However, I can modernize their version of it.
(Takes out large white silk handkerchief and in a knightly manner, spreads it out for her to walk upon - kneeling and extending his left hand to her.)

Bess.

(Taking his hand.)
Oh! Sir Alec, how thoughtful of you.
(With prim and comically royal manner she is about to X. on tiptoe.)

Alec.

Oh! Queen, come down on your entire foot.
(She passes over the handkerchief a la Raleigh and Elizabeth and goes well down R. He takes up handkerchief and presses it to his heart.)
It shall never be washed again.

Bess.

Where were you all the afternoon?

Alec.

Detained at the Hoffman House.

Bess.

Why do you go there so much?

Alec.

A fellow wouldn't be in the swim at all if he didn't stop at the Hoffman on his way up town.

Bess.

Is the food better there than anywhere else?

Alec.

You'd think so, to see the fellows sitting around the tables striking matches. Besides you get a whole art gallery thrown in.

Bess.

Like the Eden Musee?

Alec.

Yes, only the figures are moving.

Bess.

What do they do?

Alec.

Principally raise their hands to their mouths. And Bess, while you take your little fizz, and look at the pictures--

Bess.

Fizz?

(S T O P M U S I C)

Alec.

I mean as you look at the pictures, your phiz, is turned that way.

Bess.

Slang.

Alec.

We fellows all use it down town. Have to. They wouldn't understand you if you spoke English below Canal Street.

Bess.

Is the Art Gallery very beautiful?

Alec.

One picture there worth ten thousand dollars.

Bess.

What's the subject?

Alec.

Oh! Er -- a beach scene-- lot of folks going in bathing-- just like Long Branch, or Narragansette Pier, at the height of the season. You see - I - can't exactly explain it to Ladies-- when ladies go there, you stand very silent, you look at it, and then you all pass on, as if you hadn't seen it. (X'ing R.) Now Bess, when you are my wife--

Bess.

I haven't said I would be yet.

Alec.

Well, say, will you?

Bess.

Oh, I must have time to think.

Alec.

You are too young to think. Nobody ever thinks now, when they get married. Come! say "yes" and be done with it.

Bess.

Well-- yes. How long will we have to wait?

Alec.

Only till I make a million or two.

Bess.

Can't we get married till then?

Alec.

Not in New York.

Bess.

Well, brother John in his sermons, says we ought to deny ourself. I could live in Brooklyn.

Alec.

(Staggering) And I cross that river, twice a day?

Bess.

We'd be as happy as Hero and Leander. I'll be Hero, and you, Leander.

Alec.

Excuse me, Bess, not in this climate.

(Enter Dick R. U. E. and comes down R. C.)

Bess.

Oh! Dick!

Dick.

Ah! Little one!

Bess.

(Displaying her dress) How do you like it?

Dick.

Oh, exquisite.
(Holding her hands and regarding her affectionately)
But it doesn't compare with the loveliness of my little sister

(W A R N  M U S I C)

Alec.

Mr. Van Buren, that was a terrible shaking up you gave the old man to-day. Oh, we don't call you the Earthquake for nothing. When I saw Mr. Cruger hanging over the ticker in the office and making the air blue, in an undertone, I unloaded my two shares Kankaka and Okahalla preferred to Auntie

Dick.

Had you been carrying half a million, I suppose it would have made no difference?

Alec.

Only instead of Auntie supporting me, I should now be supporting Auntie.

(M U S I C)

Bess.

Wouldn't that be good of him?

Dick.

Worthy of Alexander the Great.

Bess.

(Going to L.1.E.)
Come Alec! That's our dance. Judge Knox is looking for a couple to fill the set.

Alec.

(Going R.) He can't get us. We'll go round by way of the box and get as far away from him as possible.

Bess.

Why are you afraid of Judge Knox?

Alec.

Oh, Bess! I'm in an awful fix.

(Exit Bess and Alec R.1/E. quickly.)

Dick.

(Looking after Bess.)

Ah, little Bess, you are the one thing on this earth that makes me now and then forget business. If you could as easily make me forget Phyllis Lee! Ah, I have enough on my mind without that. I came here for work - Had the Exchange been open but one hour longer to-day! But I made Cruger feel my power, and to-night he's in a condition to listen to me.

(Enter Franklin Cruger L.1.E.)

Cruger.

Ah, Van Buren - just on my way to the smoking room to have a cigar. By the way, pleasant little shock that was you gave us to-day.

Dick.

A few more like it will shake some of the names off the office doors down town.

Cruger.

(Dryly) Very cleverly done-- join me in a smoke? You might give me a few points.

Dick.

I will -- to-morrow.

Cruger.

Van Buren, I like your grit. The fight went your way to-day because I held in my reserves. But now that you have combined with Campbell in Chicago, and McVeigh in St. Louis to push me to the wall, I mean to sweep you into oblivion.

Dick.

It can't be done, Mr. Cruger, it can't be done, sir. Until I came into the street you feared no man. All feared you. Now you with the rest fear me. One firm after another has gone to pieces under my touch. You are the only man that blocks my way., And do you think I'll stop? I have no religion, no God, but one ambition-- to be master of that Street.

Cruger.

My sole aim in life is money. Show me how I can make more than I do now, and I'll abdicate in your favor.

Dick.

My only regret is, that I must fight against the father of Ann Cruger.

Cruger.

Why, what has that to do with it?

Dick.

I love her.

Cruger.

Love Ann!

Dick.

Yes.

Cruger.

Well, well, well! Does Ann know it?

Dick.

I can't ask a woman to be my wife when I'm trying to ruin her father.

Cruger.

Why not? It's business. Besides it would tie your hands and give me a little rest. But Ann may not love you.

Dick.

She may not be indifferent when she sees the advantage that must come to us all.

Cruger.

You never lose a trick do you? Well, I'll do all I can to help you, Dick, for, as son-in-law, I look upon you as a devilish good investment.

Dick.

(Aside) Once his partner I shall soon stand alone.
~~(Dick retires up R. C. - takes glass of water from water cooler.)~~ If Phyllis does not understand the meaning of my neglect, she shall [illegible] Exit [illegible]

Bess.

(Outside) Mr. Cruger!
(Enter Bess excitedly R. 1. E.)

Bess.

Oh, Mr. Cruger, come to Alec.

Cruger.

What's the trouble?

Bess.

We were dancing way on the farther side of the ball-room when Judge Knox spied him. He was coming towards us, and Alec ran and hid in box L.

Cruger.

What's he been doing to the Judge?

Bess.

(Dragging him towards R.)

Oh! He's in an awful fix.

~~(Enter Ann Cruger L. 1. E. with Creighton. She does not see Dick. Creighton bows to Ann - joins Dick at back and exits with him.)~~

Exit with Cruger R.I.E. (S T O P M U S I C)

Ann.

Papa, will you ask some one to bring me a cup of hot bouillon?

Cruger.

(Starting to go R.)

Certainly.

Ann.

No - No - no - I-- I think I'll take an ice.

(Fanning herself vigorously.)

I think I'm going to have a chill.

Cruger.

Well, you will, if you fan yourself like that.

Ann.

Oh, I mean a fever. Can't you understand, when I say chill I mean fever? (Pathetically.) Papa, why will you worry me so?

Cruger.

(Coming towards her.)

Ann, what's been the trouble with you lately?

Ann.

Have you noticed anything?

Cruger.

Noticed? When a girl wants to take an ice-cream with hot bouillion? You haven't been yourself since Christmas and to-night—

Ann.

~~To-night, you dear old papa, I never felt happier than I am~~ to-night.

Cruger.

(Laughing) I am very glad to hear that.

Bess.

Mr. Cruger please hurry or Alec will have a conniption fit before we get there.

(Exit Bess R. 1. E. greatly disturbed, holding Cruger's hand. Cruger laughing.)

Dick.

(Comes down C.) Ann.

Ann.

(Turning) Ah, Dick!

Dick.

Have you a place for me on your card? I only came here to-night, for the pleasure of one dance with you.

Ann.

I know how to take your compliments, Dick. (Handing card) Your mother tells me she has hardly spoken a word to you since you came back from Europe.

Dick.

If she didn't come to my room sometimes late at night, after I get home, I'm afraid she would never see me.

Ann.

And you have such a lovely visitor at the Rectory.

Dick.

You mean--?

Ann.

Phyllis Lee.

Dick.

John tells me, she is a very charming girl. Is she here to-night?

Ann.

Yes. She and Bess came with your brother.

(WARM MUSIC)

Dick.

Then I shall meet her.

(Handing back card)

Shall I take you back to the ball-room?

Ann.

Don't mind me. I'm going into our box to rest.

Dick.

(Aside) Very well. If Phyllis does not understand the meaning of my neglect, she shall to-night.

(Exit L. 1. E. waltz heard.)

(M U S I C)

Ann.

Oh, I wish this ball were over. How can I laugh any more? with this pain in my heart. I've tried to think only of John's happiness; but the love that God put into my heart, I cannot conquer. From the time we were playmates, he has been part of my life. Why did I let myself believe it would last always? His great love goes to her. Only friendship for me. And I am to find in my heart a place for her. I've tried, I've tried but I can't.

(Looking towards the ball-room.)

There she is. Everyone has some kind word for her. Of if I could only hear something bad about her.

(Frightened at the thought.)

God grant that the temptation does not come to me, for she is taking him out of my life and I am only a woman.

(Exit R. U. E.)

Enter Judge Knox L. 1. E. wearing badge of reception Committee, on his right breast.)

Judge.

Two more weeks like the past and I shall become a howling maniac.

(Badge comes off and drops on floor - he stoops and picks it up.)

Confound that badge! If I hadn't been on the committee on the Charity Ball for the past twenty years, I shouldn't be here to-night.

(Looking off into ball-room.)

The most remarkable thing about it is, that she moves with perfect ease. I must interrogate Alexander further on the subject. I wonder where he disappeared to! Christmas day I managed to strugle through the dinner. I don't know what I ate. I was trying to avoid looking at Mrs. De Peyster. Every time she moved, I imagined I could hear it squeak. Dinner over, I made my excuses. The next morning I was on the limited express bound for Chicago. Two days afterwards,

she accepted me by letter. She has made our engagement public and to-night I have been congratulated by dozens of people. Here's a dilemma! Linked for life to a fraction of a woman. After two weeks of investigation I find that even Chicago cannot grapple with a case like this.

(Badge falls)

Damn that badge!

(Picks it up and puts it in R. vest pocket.)

(S T O P  M U S I C)

Cruger.

(Enters R. 1. E. - Chuckling.)

Brainy old Knox to be hoaxed like this! When Alec told me I thought I should expire. There he is. I'll put him out of his misery. (Aloud) Ah, Judge---

Judge.

(With a sigh) Ah, how are you- Cruger - How are you?

Cruger.

Why, what's the matter?

Judge.

Oh! Nothing, nothing!

Cruger.

You seem troubled.

Judge.

(With forced gayety.)

Oh! No! no! I'm gleesome-- I'm airy!

Cruger.

Oh, no that won't do! I've known you too long for you to try to deceive me. There's something on your mind.

Judge.

(Absently.) Yes, cork.

Cruger.

Cork, Knox?

Judge.

Did I say Cork? I'm getting lightheaded.

Cruger.

(Aside) How the deuce shall I broach the subject? (Aloud) From your allusions, Knox, I infer that you have become attorney for some-- er-- cork trust.

Judge.

(Flaring up quickly)
What do you mean by that? What do you mean by that?

Cruger.

Why, Judge?

Judge.

I consider that personal, sir.

Cruger.

I simply want to tell you something in reference to your engagement.

Judge.

I don't want to hear it.

Cruger.

But you ought to know.

Judge.

I don't want to know, I know too much already. You're already chaffing me. I won't have it, sir.

Cruger.

Now mind, while I don't approve of what has been done--

Judge.

Approve? What the devil has that got to do with it? You don't think I am going to ask your consent to my marriage, do you?

Cruger.

No, but hear me out, and you will agree with me, that the joke is—

Judge.

Joke! How dare you allude to it as a joke? It's no joke, I'm in misery.

Cruger.

Misery?

Judge.

(Aside) Oh, I must be careful or I shall betray my bride.

Cruger.

Now listen to me and have a good laugh.

Judge.

(Solemnly) Ha-ha-ha- I shall never laugh again!

Cruger.

But I insist.

Judge.

Oh, yes, that's like you stock brokers. You expect a man to laugh at your funny stories with damnation staring him in the face. Oh, I know. I had a Wall Street experience once.

Cruger.

Perhaps you were not in the right company.

Judge.

Oh! Yes, I was.

Cruger.

What were you? A bear?

Judge.

No.

Cruger.

A bull?

Judge.

No.

Cruger.

Oh! a lamb?

Judge.

No.

Cruger.

Well, what were you then?

Judge.

An ass!

(Cruger laughs heartily.)

Thank Heaven, you're all going to the same place. And, Cruger, you'll get a red hot corner.

Cruger.

Do you think there'll be any left when you lawyers have been provided for?

Judge.

Oh, we lawyers can take care of ourselves.

Cruger.

Yes, you're better known there.

Judge.

But we're being fast crowded out by you monopolists!

Cruger.

Only let me make a corner and when you and I meet, you'll find me smiling.

Judge.

I generally do. I suppose you old boys of the street will get together and form an ice-cream and linen duster trust.

Cruger.

You don't mean to say that we stock brokers are all bound that way?

Judge.

(Crossing R.) No, but your chances are damned good.

Cruger.

Well, I'll be hanged if I tell him at all now. I'm sorry for Alec but if I'm to roast I'll keep Knox in a stew.
(Aloud) Well, I give it up, I give it up. All jokes aside, I congratulate you upon your engagement. Confidentially, now, when Mrs. De Peyster returned from Paris this time, I knew she would take steps to win you. (Judge winces.) Ha, ha, ha I'd have taken a good deal to have seen you throw yourself at her feet. (Judge winces.)

Judge.

Feet! What are rights and lefts to her?

Cruger.

Ah, here she comes.

Judge.

(Starts) Eh?
(Enter Mrs. D. Peyster L. 1. E.)

Mrs. D. P.

Ah! Mr. Cruger, and Judge Knox, too.

Judge.

(Aside) Now to look at her, who would imagine that she has a drawback?

Cruger.

I'm glad you came out here. The Judge is a little downcast to-night. I've been trying to buoy him up. (Judge winces) Ha-ha-ha, no doubt you will succeed better. Ha-ha-ha!

(Exit L. 1. E. Chuckling.)

Judge.

(Aside) I hope Dick Van Buren will get that man in a corner to-morrow and pound the life out of him.

Mrs.D.P.

Judge, it is two weeks since I've seen you, Judge, and with the exception of a hasty "how do you do" to-night you haven't spoken a word to me.

Judge.

Well you see, my duties on the committee are such that I am constantly on the hop, step, and jump as it were.

(Aside, as she comes forward.)

She doesn't even limp.

Mrs. D.P.

One would imagine that you had forgotten Christmas afternoon.

Judge.

Oh, no- I shall never forget it.

Mrs. D.P.

If you hadn't been called away so abruptly after dinner, I would have relieved your anxiety.

Judge.

Well, I felt that I must go to Chicago.

Mrs. D.P.

Oh! the look you gave me as you rushed from the room! Meissonier, would have taken you as a model, for mad Lear in the storm. I never realized until that night what a head you had.

Judge.

(Aside) She ought to have seen it the next morning.

Mrs.D.P.

I awoke early. My broker rang me up-- I connect with him by telephone you know. But I shut him off. Quotations had no charm for me that day. I confided what you had said to me to Polly.

Judge.

Polly!

Mrs. D. P.

Yes, my baby parrot. Mr. De Peyster's first present to me.

Judge.

Oh!

Mrs. D. P.

She understood every word I said.

Judge.

Indeed!

Mrs. D. P.

And what do you think she did?

Judge.

I don't know. What?

Mrs. D. P.

Nodded her head and winked her eye. A trick, Mr. De Peyster taught her, whenever he wanted me to say "yes" to anything.

Judge.

Then you accepted me on the recommendation of that bird?

Mrs. D. P.

Yes.

Judge.

(Aside) I'd like to twist Polly's neck!

Mrs. D. P.

But I'm so glad you're back. I wanted some advice! Ever since Dick Van Buren's return, United Western has been rising and falling in a manner to bewilder one. I was carrying a--- block. After selling at 92 1-3 stock-- jumped four points. I bought heavily. There was a drop of six then eight points. A terrible slump, and if I hadn't dipped into oil, I shouldn't have glided out with so good a balance.

(During this speech Mrs. De Peyster walks back and forth, the Judge in the meantime trying to see her feet.)

Judge.

(Aside) I have it. I will object to her stock jobbing, perhaps she'll discard me. (Aloud) If there is one thing that I strenuously oppose, it is to a woman in stocks.

Mrs.D.P.

Oh, I couldn't exist if I didn't dabble in stocks-- just a little.

Judge.

No - no - I could never permit it.

Mrs.D.P.

Peter!

Judge.

No - no - no - I stand upon that with both feet.
(Checks himself suddenly and turns up stage.)

Mrs.D.P.

Oh! But I will. And when I put my one foot down--

Judge.

(Aside) She alludes to it.

Mrs.D.P.

Why, should you object?

Judge.

Well, imagine my feelings some evening, in passing through the lobby of the Windsor Hotel, to hear one of those stock brokers confiding to a brother be-ar, that he had Mrs. Knox in a corner that day and squeezed her.

Mrs.D.P.

Only a figure of speech.

(WARN MUSIC)

Judge.

Oh, I object to have my wife hugged in any manner by a member of the Stock Exchange.

Mrs.D.P.

You are unnecessarily severe.

Judge.

Oh, I know them, Oh, I know 'em!

Mrs. D. P.

This is delicious!

Judge.

Delicious - It is outrageous - you must give up stocks, madam, or give me up.

Mrs.D.P.

I would give up everything in the world, Peter, sooner than give up you.

Judge.

That settles it (Aside) We are doomed to be a matrimonial tripod.

(R I N G M U S I C)

Mrs.D.P.

Why, where are you wearing your badge?

Judge.

I don't know, I don't know!

Mrs.D.P.

(Taking the badge from the Judge's pocket and pinning it on his coat.)

Oh, listen to that music! Isn't it enchanting!

(Swaying in time with the music.)

You haven't asked me to dance yet, Peter.

Judge

Do you-- dance?

Mrs.D.P.

Why, do I dance? What a question.

Judge.

How do you manage it?

Mrs.D.P.

Manage? Manage what?

Judge.

Well, with only one-- er-- er-- that is, when er-- you haven't got-- er-- both-- that is with only one good one-- you know.

Mrs.D.P.

What is the matter with you Peter? Oh, listen to the waltz, Oh, listen to the waltz. Isn't it charming!

(Makes a slight movement in time with the music.)

Judge.

(Watching her a moment, paralyzed.)

Great Heaven! She has wound it up.

Mrs.D.P.

Peter, you shall dance this with me.

(Taking hold of him.)

Come, let us join the others in the ball-room.

Judge.

(Aside) I wonder which side it's on. I want to keep out of its way.

(They exeunt L. 1. E.)

Bess.

(Enters R. Crosses and looks off L. 1. E. looking off R.)

Poor Alec! He doesn't dare come out of the box. I wonder where Judge Knox is. There he is. Oh! he fell down.

(Enter Cruger followed by Creighton L 1. E. both laughir

Cruger.

(Laughing) Poor Knox!

Creighton.

(Laughing) Why didn't you tell him?

Cruger.

(Crossing R.) He wouldn't let me. This is my second attempt to reach the smoking room. Come, Creighton, you like a good cigar.

(Enter Dick L. 1. E.)

Dick.

(Looking off into ball-room - aside.)

She came towards me just now, and I pretended not to see her.

(Enter Bess L. U. E.)

Bess.

(Coming down) Oh! Look at you, "Three Bonanzas"! I've an idea. Kitty Ives -- made a lot of money the other night at the Orthopedic Hospital, selling flowers for charity. So I'll sell a dance for charity. There's a poor family named Mattheson. The father's very ill. I told them all about the Charity Ball and to-morrow I want to take them just a little memento of it.

Cruger.

And you mean to raise it by selling a dance?

Bess.

Um -- Um. How much will you give?

Creighton.

Twenty dollars.

Cruger.

Twenty-five.

Bess.

How much will you give Dick?

Dick.

For a dance with you, Bess? Fifty.

Bess.

Oh, let's have a regular auction.
(Creighton goes up to R. U. E. and gets chair; brings it down L. C. for Bess. Then comes down C.)

Alec.

(Enters R. 1. E.)
While I was sitting in Box L. waiting, who should come in but Auntie and Judge Knox. She was trying to persuade him to continue dancing but he wouldn't.

Cruger.

Alec, I'm afraid it's going to be more difficult to get you out of this scrape than I thought.

Alec,

I told Mr. John Van Buren. He's gone to box L to explain to the Judge. Oh! If I ever get out of this I'll go to Sunday School. Hello! What's up?

Bess.

(On Chair), Selling a dance for charity, Alec, last bid fifty dollars. How much will you give-- fifty-- fifty--

(S T O P  M U S I C)

Alec.

I don't know whether I'll be spared to dance it, but fifty-one---

Creighton.

Fifty-two.

Cruger.

Fifty-three.

Dick.

Fifty-four.

Bess.

Oh-- isn't it jolly! Fifty-four-- four-- four--

Creighton.

Fifty-five.

Dick.

Sixty.

Cruger.

Sixty-five.

Alec.

(Aside) These monarchs represent millions. What show do I stand?

Bess.

Sixty-five-- and a-- five, and a five--

Alec.

I must have that dance.

Bess.

This is exciting, sixty-five!

Alec.

(Going L.) Hold the bid open till I strike Auntie.

Bess.

Bid now.

Alec.

(Going R.) I've got one share Pocomoke Canal Company-- worth sixty-eight on the street today. Be worth forty-eight to-morrow. I'll unload to Auntie to-night.

Bess.

Come, gentlemen, sixty-five! Sixty-five!

Alec.

And a half.

Bess.

An 'alf! An 'alf! An 'alf!

Dick.

Six--ty six.

Cruger.

Seventy!

Creighton.

Seventy-five.

Cruger.

Eighty.

Alec.

(Aside) I'll hock my camera but I'll have that dance.
(Aloud) Eighty-five.

Dick.

I bid ninety.

Creighton.

I bid ninety-five.

Cruger.

I bid one hundred.

Alec.

(Going L.) I bid good evening. (Meets Dick)

Dick.

Stay, Alec, I'll buy it for you. Alec Robinson bids one hundred and fifty dollars

Bess.

(Who has kept the bid going through the dialogue, with a grand flourish, before Cruger and Creighton can bid, brings sale to a sudden end. Enter John Van Buren L.U.E.)

Sold to Alexander Robinson for one hundred and fifty— Brother John!

(Jumps down from chair and runs off R. 1. E. Everybody laughs.)

John.

I seem to have caused a panic with the auctioneer. What has gone to Alec Robinson for one hundred and fifty dollars?

Cruger.

She was selling a dance for the benefit of some poor family. Mattheson, I think the name is.

John.

Then, they'll need the money sooner than she thinks. When I called this afternoon the father was very sick.

Alec.

(Aside) I'm afraid to ask him what happened in box L.

Cruger.

(To John) Well, I'm glad to find you here. It isn't every clergyman that would appear at the Charity Ball.

John.

It would be a strange sort of charity that a clergyman could not countenance. It is sufficient to me that the good women of our land are at the head of the work.

Alec

Mr. Van Buren, you've given the ladies a grand send-off. I think you could move anybody. Did you- did you- touch the Judge's heart?

John.

(With his hand around Alec's shoulder, good naturedly.)

Oh! yes, he was so glad to hear that it wasn't true, that he forgave you at once.

(Looking off R.)

But he's coming this way, he'll tell you himself.

Alec.

No - I think not, to-night. I'll let him alone for a few days.

(Exit L. 1. E. hastily.)

Judge.

(Enter R. 1. E. radient.)

She is without a flaw.

Cruger.

Well I could have told you that.

Judge.

But you took precious good care not to.

Cruger.

At least permit me to congratulate you upon the additional member of your family.

(W A R N  M U S I C)

Judge.

Cruger, bah! John, if I hadn't received the information from anyone but you, I should annihilate the young hoaxter.

(Enter Mrs. De Peyster L. 1. E.)

Mrs.D.P.

Judge, after your fall you remained in box L. so long that I became alarmed.

Judge.

Ah, forgive me. Allow me to make amends. Put me down for every dance left on your card?

Mrs.D.P.

Oh, no! It might affect you as the waltz did.

( M U S I C )

Judge.

Oh, I feel better now, I feel as if I could indulge in a Highland fling! (Dancing) Tee- del- de- del - de---

Mrs. D.P.

Oh, Judge - I beg of you--

Cruger.

Jubilant, isn't he?

Judge.

(Giving his arm to Mrs.D.P.)

I feel as buoyant as a cargo of cork.

(Glaring at Cruger.)

With the emphasis on cork.

(Exeunt Judge and Mrs. De Peyster L. 1. E.)

(Dick who during the above has been seen to turn faint has gone up to the settee L. C. and thrown himself on it At this moment in the midst of the laughter he is seen by John with his head resting back against the window-sill, his eyes closed.)

John.

(Goes to him quickly)

Dick! Dick!

Cruger.

What's the matter?

Creighton.

(Who has followed John up to him and assists him down stage.)

Shall I get you a doctor?

Dick.

(Sinking into chair L. C.)

Doctor? No! Can't a man seek a breath of fresh air without a doctor?

Creighton.
I think I had better get one.

Dick.
(Starting to his feet angrily and crossing R.)
No, no- I say- I'm engaged to Miss Cruger for the next dance and I mean to dance it.

Cruger.
You'll have to be more careful, Dick, or that little scheme of ours will never be consummated.

Dick.
It will, Mr. Cruger, - it will - and I'll begin my part of it to-night.

Cruger.
Well, I wish you luck. You'll have to get a doctor for me if I don't get a smoke soon- Come Creighton - come.
(Exeunt Cruger R. 1. E. followed by Creighton)

John.
You ought not to be here to-night.

Dick.
This! Nothing. (Intensely) To-day's work with Cruger was worth it.
(He shakes with the intensity of his feeling.)

John.
See how it has shattered your nerves, blanched your face. Why Dick, I'm only thirty-five and you are twice my age at thirty-two.

Dick.
(Laying his hand on John's shoulder.)
Nonsense - old fellow, you're wrong.
(Holding out his hand.)
Look! No shattered nerves there. I wish I could make you understand how different your work is from mine. Why don't you let me have my own way?

John.
Because you are taking from me the companion who never had a joy or a sorrow that his brother did not share.

Dick.
We are not boys now. What do you want me to do?

John.

Give me back my brother Dick.

Dick.

I shall soon rid you of anxiety. I am to become Franklin Cruger's son-in-law.

John.

You marry Ann Cruger!

Dick.

(RL C.) Yes, why shouldn't I?

John.

(C.) Christmas night I found you in your room, with your head bowed upon a letter. You told me it came from a woman that you loved. Was it Ann Cruger?

Dick.

(Hesitates) No.

John.

Yet you speak of marriage with her.

Dick.

Men in my position can't consult their hearts.

John

And what will become of that other woman?

Dick.

Oh, she'll get over it.

John.

(Reproachfully) Dick! You love her and she-- God help her -- loves you.

Dick.

I-- I won't talk about her--

John.

In this race for supremacy you don't even stop at the breaking of a human heart.

Dick.

(Angrily) John!

(Enter Phyllis L. 1. E.)

Phyllis.

(To John) Mr. Van Buren--

(Sees Dick, and stops.)

Dick.

(Bowing) Miss Lee.

John.

Well, I declare. Living under the same roof and you hardly know each other. Dick I blame you for that.

Dick.

(To Phyllis) I regret that I have not been able to visit my home as much as I should wish since Miss Lee came here. (Crosses L.) I must return to the ball room. You will excuse me?

(Bows and exits L. I. E.)

John

(Aside) The look that was in her face the day I first saw her. (To Phyllis) I hope I did right in asking you to come to-night?

Phyllis.

Don't think me ungrateful, Mr. Van Buren - I realize how patient you have been with me.

John.

More than once of late, I've noticed that you are troubled about something. Why, even now there is a frightened look in your face. What have you to fear?

Phyllis.

I try to feel that there is nothing to fear, but--

(Turning her eyes towards the ball-room.)

Oh, but I can't!

John.

Do you fear the future when I tell you that nothing shall harm you?

Phyllis.

Even when you tell me.

(Enter Bess L.I.E.)

Bess.

Brother John, there's a messenger for you from Mrs. Mattheson - He's waiting in the corridor.

(Enter Ann R. 1. E.)

John.

I'm afraid her husband must be worse - Ann - won't you remain with Miss Lee? I shan't be long.

(Apart to Ann)

You couldn't have come at a more opportune moment.

If His great love goes to her, only friendship for me and I am to find a place in my heart for her, I've tried! I've tried!! but I can't,
(Starts to go R.U.E.)

Phyllis.

Mr. Van Buren- as it will be late when you return, I suppose there will be no lamp in the window to-night?

John.

Misery keeps all sorts of hours. Never a night passes that I don't put my lamp in its place. Some unfortunate who needs my help may see it and know that the door is open and I am waiting.

(Then to Ann.)

There is a sorrow in her heart that she will not tell me - you speak to her for my sake. Come Bessie!

(Exit L. I. E. with Bess.)

Ann.

(Aside) Well! This is delightful—

Phyllis.

(Aside) He does not come home because I am not there.

Ann.

(Aside) I suppose I must play the hypocrite.

(Phyllis clutches chair to support herself.)

Why, what's the matter?

(S T O P  M U S I C)

Phyllis.

Don't mind me.

Ann.

You are faint; rest here.

Phyllis.

You are so kind.

Ann.

Are you better. (Crossing L.) Shall we go back to the ball-room?

Phyllis.

(Crossing R.) No, I can't go back there.

Ann.

Why not?

Phyllis.

Oh, Miss Cruger, I can tell you, you will help me.

Ann.

Why, Miss Lee, in what do you need my help?

Phyllis.

(R. C.) I know of a woman who came into a home where everything was done for her that loving hearts could suggest. She made them believe she was worthy of their love when she was not, now she wants to tell them the truth.

Ann.

Why does she not?

Phyllis.

She is afraid.

Ann.

Of their condemnation?

Phyllis.

Of their pain at learning that they have been deceived.

Ann.

Did this woman confide in you?

Phyllis.

Yes- Those whom she is deceiving trust her implicity - yet I allow her to remain among them. What would you do in my place?

Ann.

I must know more about her.

Phyllis.

She wants to confide in you - There is no one else to whom she can go. She is utterly helpless without a home or friends

Ann.

Alone?

Phyllis.

Except for the man who said he loved her.

Ann.

Why does he not protect her?

Phyllis.

Oh God!

(W A R N  M U S I C)

Ann.

A broken promise?

Phyllis.

Yes-- she knows it now.

Ann

(Half suspicious - with a fixed look at Phyllis.)
You seem to take her case very much to heart.

Phyllis.

So would you if you knew how much she had suffered.

Ann.

To-morrow you shall take me to her.

Phyllis.

She is here to-night.

(M U S I C)

Ann.

Here, oh, be prudent. For if the people in that ball-room knew of this woman in their midst, penitent though she be--

Phyllis.

Would they not have mercy?

Ann.

Oh, I am afraid to answer. We open our purses and give our gold to the unfortunate. But when we are asked to open our hearts and give our sympathy to some poor creature who has erred-- ah! Then we draw back. Our charity stays at home locked up in our selfish hearts. But there is one person to whom this woman can go for help.

Phyllis.

And that one?

Ann.

John Van Buren.

Phyllis.

Oh, it is he who has been deceived.

Ann.

John Van Buren?

Phyllis.

Yes.

Ann.

And the woman?

Phyllis.

Myself!

Ann.

(Aside) And a moment ago I wanted to hear something bad about her.

Phyllis.

You are not like the rest of the world.

Ann.

(Aside) And this is the woman he loves?

Phyllis.

(Going to her) Help me!

Ann.

Don't! Don't touch me. There is no place here for you. I told you what we were; and I am no better than the rest.

Phyllis.

(Going up R. C.)

Let me go! Let me go!

(Enter Dick L. 1. E.)

Dick.

I have come to claim you.

(Phyllis, at the sound of Dick's voice, stops. Dick seeing her, stops.)

Ann, have you forgotten our dance?

Ann.

Dick, will you not excuse me?

Dick.

Certainly, if you wish. It's hard to give up my dance, but I suppose I must be content and ask pardon for intruding.

(About to withdraw L.)

Phyllis.

(Forgetting herself and starting to him.)

Dick!

(Ann, amazed, starts. Dick Stops. Phyllis realizing her mistake stands motionless.)

Dick.

(Turning quietly) Did you call me, Miss Lee?

Phyllis.

(Confused) No, I-- I-- I-- I forgot.

Dick.

(To Phyllis) You appear to be in some trouble.

Ann.

She is.

Dick.

(To Ann) Have you and Miss Lee been exchanging confidences?

Ann.

She has placed in my keeping the holiest confidence that one woman can give to another.

Dick.

Indeed!

Ann.

But she guards with a woman's devotion-- the name of him, who should have given her a place among his own.

Dick.

I appreciate your motive in making me the recipient of this intelligence, and I infer that she will henceforth cease to make the Rectory her home.

(W A R N M U S I C)

(Ann makes a movement toward him as though to speak.)
You wish some explanation to be made of Miss Lee's departure that will at once be generous to her and merciful to those among whom she has lived. I will render any service in my power.

Ann.

Then tell your brother that I have persuaded Miss Lee to come with me to-night to my home.

Phyllis.

You spoke the truth. There is no place for me.

Ann.

Yes, there is a place, in my arms--
(Phyllis comes to her. Ann puts her arms about her.)
close to my heart.
As Ann Cruger's friend, her departure from the Rectory needs no explanation.

# THE CHARITY BALL.

## ACT III.

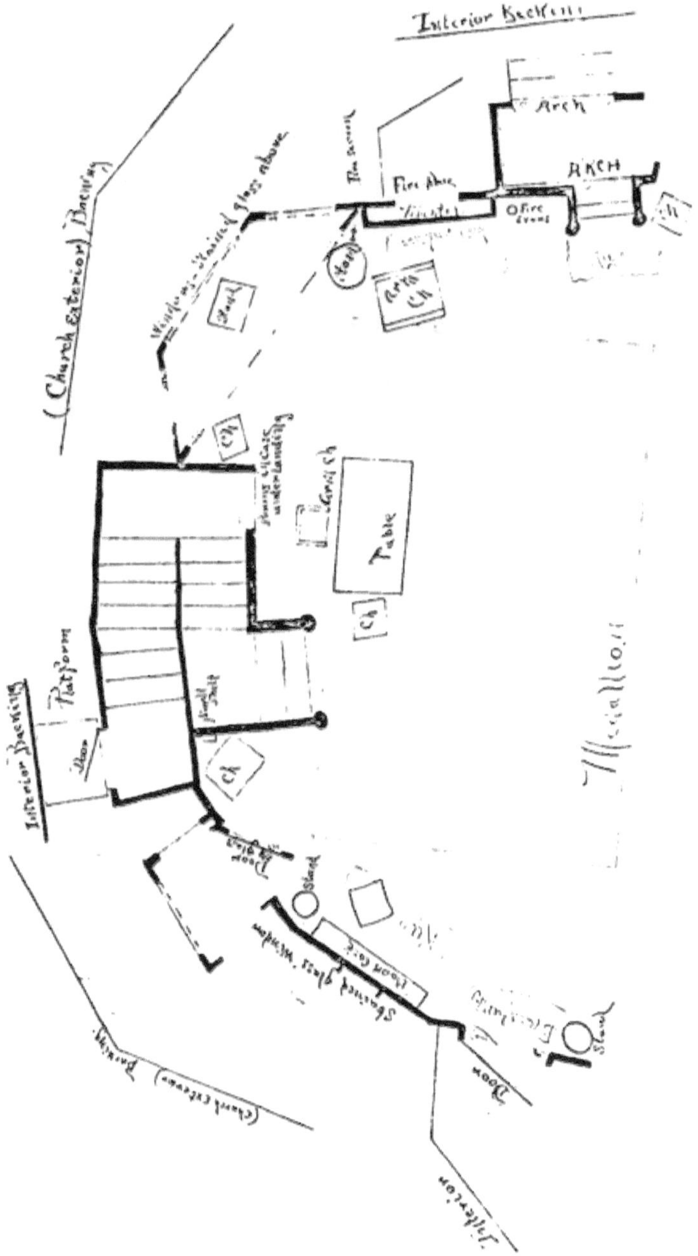

Interior Backing
Arch
ARCH
Fire Place
Fire screen
Window - stained glass above
(Church Exterior) Backing
Arm Ch
Ch
Table
Platform
Interior Backing
Door
Ch
Door
Stand
Stained glass Window
Book case
Stand
Door
(Church exterior) Backing
Interior

PROPERTY PLOT --- ACT III.

FURNITURE REQUIRED: (For arrangement see Diagram)

4 Stands. Down R.--up R. C. and two up L. C.
Book-case R. Also one under landing up C.
Writing Table C.
Arm Chair up C.
Large upholstered Arm-Chair before Fireplace L.
Odd Chair up R. C.
4 Chairs.-- R. C. - R. of table - up L. C. and down L

---///---

Floor Cloth and Medallion down. Rugs as indicated.

---///---

On Stand down R. Lighted Lamp (turned down.)
On Book-case, Several books.
On Stand R. Books.
On Table C. Writing materials, Inkstand, Papers, Pens, Sand Box, Matches, Two or three Books, Small Taper Lamp, (to Light), Candle Extinguisher, Prayer-Book.
On Stand up L. Lighted Lamp, (turned down)
On Mantel L. Clock, Two Bronze Vases, Two Fancy Candle-Sticks.

---///---

CURTAINS.

Dark Red at door R.
Soft Silk on door up R. C.
Dark Red on Arch up L. C.
Ditto on Arch down L.
Light green silk on window up R.
Light silk on bay window up L.

PICTURES:

Etchings. Two small between door and book-case, R.
Long narrow one over book-case, R.
Two small ones between door R. C. and book-case.
Large one up R. C.
Small ditto up C.
Two small ditto up L. C.
Two small ditto between window L. C. and Mantel.
Portrait, (Engraving) over mantel, L.

----------

SIDE PROPERTIES: For Sophie: Fancy Candlestick and lighted Candle. Snow bags behind all windows. Sleigh-bells Wind-machine off L.

OFF R.: Organ, Salt for Snow for John and Betts.

------:0:------

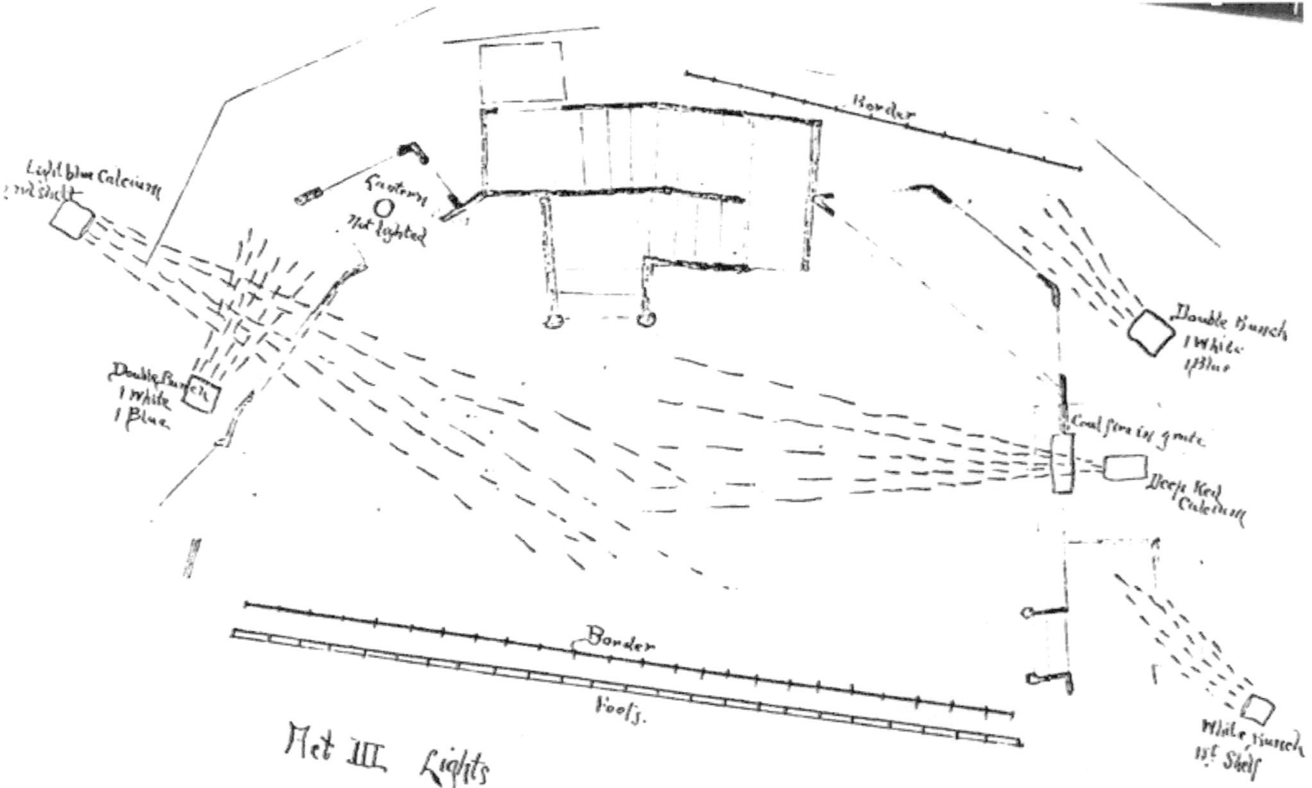


Act III Lights

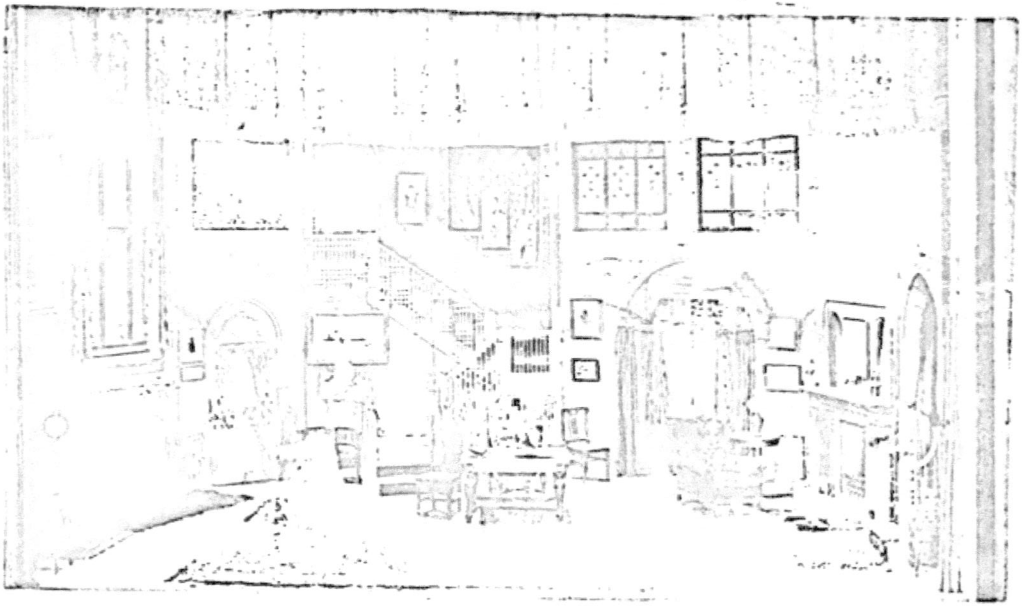

Act 3rd.

# LIGHTS --- ACT III.

---:0:---

AT RISE OF CURTAIN: Foots and Front Border off.
Black Border on 3/4.
Blue Bunce Lights R. and L.
White Bunch dow L.
Dark Red Calcium on through fireplace.

At Rise, when Sophie enters with lighted candle: Foots up 1/4.
When John extinguishes candle: Foots down.
When Phyllis comes to Window L. put White bunch on gradually. Work down gradually after she leaves window.
At Cue "Somebody's here": Blue Calcium put on, R. through window.
When John lights Candle: Foots go up 1/4.
When Dick enters: Foots up a little gradually.

House lights on 1/4 throughout act.

---oOo---

## -%- THE CHARITY BALL -%-

## ACT III.

S C E N E:- The Study at the Rectory. "In the watches of the night". For description of room and furniture see diagram. A soft sombre light relieves the darkness of the room. The cold gray light of a winters night comes through the stained glass windows at the back. Lamp used by Betts in Act I. on the table L. C. burning low. During the progress of this act, an air of stillness must prevade the stage. House lights down as low as possible. Foots and borders out. Ten seconds after curtain rises, distant sleigh bells heard gradually drawing near, until sleigh stops L.

At rise of curtain, Sophie enters L. 1. E. with candle - stage lights go up a trifle- Sophie puts candle on table and goes R.

Bess.

(Outside) Good night, Mrs. De Peyster, much obliged.

Mrs.D.P.

(Outside) Good night, my dear.

Bess.

(Outside) Good night, Judge Knox.

Judge.

(Outside) Good night, little one.

Alec.

(Outside) Good night, Bess, pleasant dreams.

Bess.

(Crossing R. Outside) Same to you, Alec, good night. (During the above, Sophie L. with lighted candle, and opens door R. 1. E. Sleigh heard to drive off, and the sound to die away in the distance. Foots and Borders go up one-fourth when Sophie enters with candle.)

Mrs.D.P., Judge, Alec, Bess.

Good night!

(Bess entering R. 1. E. wrapped in furs, runs to the fire)

Bess.

Thanks, Sophie. Close the door quick. B-r-r-r-! (Sitting before fire) Come help me get off my things. (Sophie closes door and comes to her.)

Mrs.V.B.

(Outside L.) Is that you, Bess?

Bess.

Yes, Angel, are you up?

(During this, Bess is seated in Arm-chair by fire, and Sophie kneeling beside her takes off her overshoes, and leggins.)

Mrs. Van.B.

(Outside). Do you think I could go to bed and you not home? Didn't your brother John come with you?

Bess.

No, he was called away quite early, and he left me in charge of Mrs. De Peyster. I came home with an engaged couple.

Mrs. Van B.

Oh! Then Judge Knox was with you?

Bess.

Um -- um. And Alec.

Mrs. Van B.

(Outside) Phyllis, what makes you so silent to-night. (A second's pause)

Bess.

Phyllis isn't here, Angel.

Mrs. Van B.

(Outside) Not here? Where is she, then?

Bess.

She went home with Ann Cruger. They left before we did. (Jumping up from chair and giving Sophie her opera cloak) Take 'em up stairs Sophie. Oh, I've had such a lovely time.

(Exits Sophie L. 3. E.)

There's brother John now. (Runs to balustrade) Angel, here' brother John. Wait for me a minute. I've something very important to tell him.

Mrs. Van B.

(Outside) Can't you wait till morning?

Bess.

No, it won't keep.

Mrs. Van B.

(Outside) Ha, ha, ha! Very well, very well.

Bess.

I just couldn't sleep if I didn't tell 'em both I was engaged to Alec.

(Enter John R. 1. E. He wears a cape over-coat, and high hat, both of which are slightly covered with snow.)

Brother John.

John.

(Removes coat and hat, which he places on chair up R. C.)

Why, Bess, you here?

Bess.

Yes, Brother John; I wanted to tell you something. Ann sent word to you that Phyllis was going to spend the night with her

John

She went home with Ann?

Bess.

Yes. So you were not to expect her at the Rectory -- And Brother John there's something else I want to tell you. If you approve, Angel is sure to.

John.

(Coming down to her)

Oh! You want to fix matters with me first, eh?

Bess.

If you please, Brother John. It's so much easier to win your big brother over, than it is your little mother.

John.

(Taking her face betwen her hands)

Well, what mischief have you been up to?

Bess.

(Returning his look) Been getting engaged.

John.

Engaged?

Bess.

Um -- um. (Shyly) In a sort of a kind of a way -- you know - Alec, and I have been planning to-night how we'd arrange matters when we were married.

John.

Indeed! You've gone so far as that?

Bess.

Couldn't go any further till we saw you and Angel.

John.

Yes, yes; but, you are both so young.

Bess.

Oh, we'll outgrow that. Brother John, Alec wants to give me an engagement ring. You'll let him, won't you? Say yes, and this will be the happiest moment I ever lived.

John.

(Caressing her hair) I remember you said the same thing the day when you put on your first long dress.

Bess.

But that long dress just revolutionized me.

John.

Go nestle this little head on your mother's breast; tell her of your love. Listen to what she says. This is one of the cases where the little mother, can give better advice than the big brother. Go to her.

Bess.

(Goes up steps L. 1. E. turns and speaks) Brother John!

(He comes to her; she kisses him)

I thought it was great fun getting engaged. But it's not. (Making a wry face) I want to - cr--cry. (Exit L.E.)

John.

What is sweeter to hear than a young girl's first confession of her love.

(John turns up lamp on table L. and places it in alcove window at back. Church clock strikes two. He comes to book-case and is about to take down book when there is heard a knock at chapel door R. 1. E.)

Come in!

(Enter Betts R.I.E. wrapped in overcoat and huge comforter, slightly covered with snow. John takes book and sits behind table.)

Betts.

(Singing) "Out in the cold world, out in the street". Pretty severe storm this, Mr. Van Buren. Thought I would go to my room this way. Little shorter than through the Parish buildings. Been playing chess for the last two hours with old Joe Randolph. He's a good player, but law! He can't hold a candle to me -- We had a spirited argument about a certain move which he agreed to leave to you. You see my King's pawn tried to take his King's castle. By the way, how did you leave Mattheson?

John.

He died about an hour ago.

Betts.

God bless me. He was a good chess player. What in the world his poor wife will do, I don't know — with all those little children on her hands.

John.

Something must be done for them. Come to me in the morning, Betts; I shall have something for you to do.

Betts.

All right, sir, good night.

John.

Good night, Betts.

Betts.

(Going toward chapel door R.3.E. Aside) Everybody thinks I'm the most charitable man in the New York. It's all him. (At door) Shall I disturb you if I practice an anthem or two?

John.

Now, how many times a week do you want me to answer that question? Betts, when do you sleep? Morning, noon, and night you seem to be at that organ.

Betts.

Why, sir, it's part of me. Nearly forty years since I played the first anthem on it. Think of the joy and sorrow it has accompanied in that time. It's a living thing. My wife, my son, and my little girl used to listen to it. Somehow it seems to bring me nearer to them.

John.

(Taking his hand) Ah -- old friend! Many a time has your uncomplaining nature taught me how to endure.

Betts.

Sure it doesn't disturb you?

John.

Its tones are always soothing to me, and to-night more than ever, I want to hear them.

Betts.

"No one to love -- none to caress". (Exit R.3.E. singing to himself as he goes out.)

John.

How hard it is snowing. When I think of my loved ones sheltered from harm, how I pity any poor creature who may be out in such a storm. (Looking off L. 1. E.) They've gone upstairs. I could almost have asked Betts to remain here with me. I have such a feeling of unrest. Except for the storm outside everything is still. And yet the very silence of the room speaks a nameless dread. The shadows from the fire-light seem to shape themselves into shapes of warning -- all pointing at me -- I fear no foe, so why should thoughts like these oppress me.

(Leans bach supporting himself with both hands upon the table. The soft tones of the organ are heard. Lights small taper lamp from the candle, then extenguishes candle)

I will go into the church, and in the chancel where I offer up the sacrifice of praise and thanksgiving before my congregation I will pour out my heart -- alone --

(Ascends stairs R.U.E. As John reaches the first landing there is heard a tapping at the window. He pauses, his face toward the room and listens. He then ascends the steps to the second landing. Meanwhile at the window the white face of Phyllis Lee is seen, as she leans against the window frame for support. She is still in her ball dress, her wrap thrown over her, the snow falling on her partly covered head)

Phyllis.

(Feebly moaning) Mr. Van Buren! Mr. Van Buren!

John.

(Stops on second landing and listens intently) What is that?

Phyllis.

(As before) Mr. Van Buren!

John.

Is it fancy that changes the sound of the organ, into the tones of a voice calling upon me?

(Hearing nothing more, he turns and passes into the church. The darkness of the room increases as his light disappears. Phyllis leaves the window. A moment later the door R. 1. E. is opened and she staggers into the room, closes the door by falling back against it, her arms extended, clutching the portieres.)

Phyllis.

(Low) Mr. Van Buren! Mr. Van Buren! You told me when my cross was heavier than I could bear, to come to you. It is -- it is!

(Phyllis sinks down at the steps; as she lies sobbing, the sound of the organ dies away; a moment's silence broken only by an occasional sob from Phyllis. John reappears with the light.)

John.

I thought I heard a cry coming from this room.

(Phyllis utters a low plaintive moan)

Again!

(Starts to descend, when a low moan causes him to pause on the second landing)

Some one is here.

(He is coming down, when a sob at his feet stops him. He holds the light aloft as he looks down)

A woman!

(He places the light in a niche at his right and bends over her)

Some unfortunate who needs my help.

(Gently raising her, her head resting on his breast so he cannot see her face.)

My poor child, what trouble has brought you to me -- a night like this? Oh; how cold you are! Come to the fire.

(As they reach the spot where the light from the hall window falls into the room, she raises her head and looks up into his face.)

Phyllis! What is the meaning of this?

Phyllis.

I have come to tell you now what I should have confessed at first.

John.

(Hardly able to speak the words) You come to me -- at such an hour — to tell me -- what?

Phyllis.

I -- I -

John.

Speak.

Phyllis.

Oh! I want to die! (Sinking at his feet) I ant to die!

John.

(Standing breathless with apprehension) To die! Then I was not mistaken. The look I saw in your ace the day you knelt by your father's bedside -- the same that met my sight yesterday in the church -- and again in the ball-room to-night -- I knew there was a grief you were trying to tell me, but what can it be that brings you to me like this?

(At this moment the door R.I.E. is quickly opened and Ann Cruger enters. She is still in her ball-room dress, though warmly enveloped in her cloak. Ann at sight of Phyllis kneeling before John gives a half inaudible cry of despair.)

Ann.

John!

John.

Ann! (John quickly turns and lights candle on table)

Ann.

(Going to Phyllis and sinking down beside her, takes her in her arms)

Phyllis! We had just arrived home. I went to prepare her room myself, and when I came down stairs she had gone. Through this terrible storm she has walked here. John, what has she said to you?

John.

Nothing.

Ann.

(Aside -- fervently) Thank God! (Aloud) Phyllis, dear, come home with me.

Phyllis.

(Sobbing) No -- No.

Ann.

John, you placed her in my care. She is not herself. You asked me to be her friend. I beg of you be guided by me, let me take her home.

John.

There is something she wants to tell me

Ann.

She must not. You cannot help her. I may yet find the way -- John, there are times in our lives when our faith in those we trust must be absolute. Such a time has come to you and me now. Trust me and let me take her with me.

Phyllis.

It is only of myself that I will speak.

Ann.

(Aside, wringing her hands) Oh! and it was I who told her to come to him.

Phyllis

Let me tell him.

John.

I am listening.

Ann.

Wait until to-morrow.

Phyllis.

No -- no.

Ann.

John, not to-night -- not to-night.

John.

Why not to-night? She comes to me at this hour. I find her prostrate upon those steps. I hear sobs that can only come from a broken heart. I am God's minister. Why wait until to-morrow when a heart is breaking to-night? (Bending over her) Come.

Phyllis.

No, let me stay as I am.

John.

(To Phyllis tenderly) If it were any one but you, I should believe that only one misfortune could bow you to the dust like this.

Phyllis.

(Slowly raising her eyes to his) Believe it of me.

John.

(Extending his hand as though to keep back any further words she may utter)

No!

(For a moment he stands appalled, his eyes fixed upon hers. As the truth dawns upon him, he raises his eyes reverently. For a moment he looks in front of him with a dull dead stare. Then with a cry of pain he suddenly burries his face in his hands, turning his back to the audience)

Oh!

Phyllis.

What must you think of me. Do not spare me. Nothing that you can say will be as bitter as what I have said to myself every day since I have been here. I thought it would all come right. I believed so in him. And I waited --- waited.

(At this moment the organ is heard playing softly the prelude to the anthem Phyllis, after a slight pause, turns to Ann)

Ann.

Phyllis!

Phyllis.

What is left for me now.

Ann.

Hands that will uphold you. Hearts that will enfold you with their love!

Phyllis.

Everybody will despise me.

(Betts is heard singing the words "He was despised")

Ann.

My arms are opened to you.

Phyllis.

They will turn me from their doors.

(Betts heard singing "Despised and Rejected")

Ann.

My home shall be yours.

(Ann has slowly raised her head listening to the anthem)

Because one man has been pitiless, do you think he who reads our hearts will not see all that is pure in yours?

(John turns toward them, his face grief-stricken, his eyes bent sadly on Phyllis. Organ dies away)

John.

Phyllis, tell me. The one to whom you gave your heart---?

Phyllis.

I am his, until I die. Even beyond the grave he will have my love.

John.

(After a slight pause) Then all may yet be right. It must be. No man can be indifferent to such a love. How deep that love is, he shall learn from me.

Phyllis.

You?

John.

No longer the man you have known. Not even the priest. It is your brother, who speaks to you now. I will meet him face to face, and make him render an account to me.

Dick.

(Outside L. 1. E.) John, are you there?

(Phyllis gives a half-stifled cry. Ann rises with a look of terror)

John.

Don't be alarmed. It is only my brother Dick.

Ann.

(To Phyllis) Not a word. God help me to shield him from this blow at least. (With forced calmness) John, shall I take her with me now?

Dick.

(Outside L. 1. E.) John, are you in the study?

John.

(Holding curtains at L. 1. E.)

Yes, I am here.

(At sound of John's voice, Dick stops outside door)

Dick.

(Outside) Oh! Just a word with mother. Then I want to talk to you.

John.

I shall be here.

Ann.

Come, Phyllis. (To John) It is late and she needs rest.

John.

Before she goes, there is something else left for her to tell me -- his name.

(Dead pause)

Phyllis.

Don't let me say any more. I should have gone away and buried my sorrow, where none of you could have seen me again.

John.

Has not the hardest part been told?

Ann.

John, I beg of you don't question her any more.

John.

(To Ann) Do you know?

Ann.

Yes.

John.

Then why is she afraid to tell me? Does she remember when I stood by the bed of her dying father? He took my hand and with his other placed upon your head even as mine is now, said --"I have no one to leave my little girl to -- will you take care of her"? Do you remember what I replied? In this, your hour of need, will you not let me keep my promise?

Phyllis.

Yes; you will plead with him as I cannot. He will listen to you. I won't believe he doesn't love me. His cruel words to-night---

John.

To-night? You saw him to-night?

Phyllis.

Yes.

John.

In that ball-room?

Phyllis.

Yes, yes.

John.

Do I know him?

Ann.

(Aside) Oh! And I am powerless.

John.

Phyllis, tell me.

(Phyllis with bowed head signifies "yes." In a whisper)

I know him? Who is he?

Ann.

(Making a movement toward him) John.

John.

Who is he?

(Phyllis slowly raises her head as if about to speak)

Ann.

(With a cry turns quickly to Phyllis , and presses her lips to those of Phyllis in a long kiss)

Phyllis!

Phyllis.

(After slight pause --- turning R.)

Take me away, don't let me say any more.

(Sitting in chair R.)

John.

Why did you not let her speak?

Ann.

What you want her to say will bring pain --

John.

To whom?

(Ann raises her head with a look of supplication to John)

What is it you both know and are trying to keep from me?

(Looks toward the door at which Dick's voice was heard then at the two women.)

Phyllis, you are not strong enough at present to return home with Ann.

(Taking her hand and leading her to R.3.E.)

I want you to rest here a moment.

(He closes the door and turns to Ann. Organ heard)

If any one can make this blow less bitter, Ann, you are that one. Speak.

Ann.

I cannot --- Oh! I cannot!

John.

Because it is my brother.

(Ann, unable to reply, bows her head on her breast. With a groan he falls into the chair, his arms extended across the table.)

Ann.

(Tenderly approaching him) John!

(Kneeling by his side tearfully)

If I could only suffer for you.

John.

(His arm around her head as she looks wistfully into his face)

Always faithful! When days are darkest you are closest by my side. Whenever affliction comes you are near to soothe and comfort. You tried so hard to spare me. God, reward you!

(Pointing to chapel R.3.E.)

Go to her.

(Ann goes toward R.3.E.)

Dick.

(Outside) Ha! ha! ha! ha! No fear! I'll not keep him up long.

(John rises and stands with his eyes fixed on L.1.E.)

Ann.

(Turning) John, remember, he is your brother.

John.

(Immoveable, his eyes fixed on door) I shall not forget that she loves him. But close the door and do not interrupt us.

(Almost in a whisper)

Go!

(Ann, with a look of fear goes out R.3.E. and the door is heard to close. Enter Dick L.I.E. His manner is light and careless, his face slightly flushed with wine. He must not show the least sign of intoxication, his condition being simply that of a man exhilarated from drinking several glasses of wine)

Dick.

(Coming down steps) Hello, John. Mother didn't want me to keep you up. Why you are as great a night owl as I am.

(Comes down and brings chair from up R. down to L. of table) I've been at the club, I knew I couldn't sleep. Saw your light in the window. You keep it for the unfortunate Well, here I am.

(Throwing himself in chair L. of table)

Been in bad luck to-night.

(With dogged firmness, bringing his hand down on table)

But I'll pull through.

(Suddenly stopping and looking up --- then laughs)

There old fellow; you don't know what I'm talking about. That affair concerning Ann Cruger. I've had a little set back But her father and I had a talk after we left the Opera House.

As a man of the world he understands. Come, John, be sociable If I didn't have you to come to sometimes --- Do you know there's nothing quiets me like one of those old time talks with you.

(Looking vacantly before him)

I think you're right, old fellow. "The game isn't worth the candle". Some nights after I've been stirring things up in the cauldron down town, I come back here --- (Suddenly changing). Oh, if I'm not careful, I'll end in Bloomingdale. There's only one way out of it. It will all end the day I stand before St. Mildred's cancel rail and hear you speak the words that will make Ann Cruger my wife.

John.

(Who during the above has remained motionless, his eyes fixed on Dick)

I would sooner speak the words that consign your body to the grave.

Dick.

(Startled, looks at him) John what's the matter with you? What are you looking at me that way for? (Rising) Brother!

John.

(With calm intensity) Take it back. No one shall call me brother, whom I can call scoundrel!

Dick.

(Now entirely himself) John!

John.

Shall I tell you why you cannot sleep? Why you try to drown your thoughts in dissipation at your club? Because you cannot think of the man we both call father, and look at what you have done.

Dick.

You've discovered who the woman is ---

John.

Yes, the woman to whom I gave shelter under this roof -- and yet you said nothing.

Dick.

My interests demanded that I give her up. And I did. I am no better than the rest of men. There's no use talking about it now. With Cruger's assistance I mean to marry his daughter

John.

The world condemns a woman for one fault, yet permits a man to wreck a human life, and still thinks himself worthy to offer himself in marriage to another.

Dick.

(Angrily) John, you've said enough. What right have you to call me to account?

John.

Stop.

Dick.

You say I'm not to call you brother. What are you then, that I should listen?

John.

Conscience --- since yours is dead. A conscience against which you need not try to close your ears, for I will cry with a voice so loud, that though you shut yourself in your vaults of steel, and fortify yourself with mountains of gold, I will pierce them all until I reach your heart. Before you cross the threshold of that door, I want a promise.

Dick.

What promise?

John.

That you will make Phyllis Lee your wife.

Dick.

Impossible.

John.

She came to the house of God for refuge. His minister will see that grace is done her.

Dick.

I've determined what to do, and nothing can change me.

John.

Then I put aside my calling -- all kinship between us, and stand before you man to man. Will you make Phyllis Lee your wife?

Dick.

No!

John.

Do you know what that refusal means to her?

Dick.

Since you care so much for h r yourself ---

John.

Don't say it.

Dick.

If you love her?

John.

(Angrily raising his arm to strike him)
You-----

Mrs. V. B.

(Outside L.1.E.) Boys!
(John gradually lowers his hand)
Boys!

John.

(Apart) I now see the wisdom of God in permitting her to be blind. She cannot see the shame stamped on your face.
(Mrs. Van B. appears L.1.E.)

Mrs. Van B.

My boys, do you know what time it is? Almost three o'clock You bring your old mother to you just as you used to when you were little fellows and lie awake and talk until I came to stop you. Ah! you may be grown men to others, but you are still my boys. Now which of you shall I punish for keeping the other up so late? It's Dick's fault I'm sure. Do you remember John, night before the fourth of July, when Dick put a large fire-cracker under your bed and set it off? And when everybody in the house rushed up into your room to see what on earth had happened - you in the middle of the room frightened out of your wits, and the little rogue in bed pretending to be fast asleep. Ha! ha! ha!

John.

We were boys then, mother.

Mrs. Van B.

Yes, my coming here to-night to make you both go to bed brings it all back to me. Dick, where are you?

Dick.

(With forced laugh, crossing to her) Here, mother, here.

Mrs. Van B.

(Taking his hand) You were so quiet. I didn't know but that something was the matter.

Dick.

Dick.

(Laughing) No, no --- mother, dear.

Mrs. Van B.

Well, I'll kiss you both good night. (Kisses Dick, then John who comes to her) Oh, John, have you been telling Dick about Bess?

John.

(With an effort of calmness) No --- no.

Mrs. Van B.

Well then, I'll tell him. Dick, it seems that Bess---

(Bess's head appears from between the folds of the portiere L. 1.E.)

Bess.

Oh, Angel, please let me tell him.

Mrs. Van B.

What! you down stairs?

Bess.

(Comes down steps. She has on a dainty little night wrapper)

Yes, I couldn't sleep. I don't think I'll ever sleep again. I heard Dick's voice, and I couldn't keep under the bed clothes.

(Comes down to Dick, who sits in an arm chair before the fireplace - sits on his lap affectionately)

Dick, did you think I could tell all the others and forget you? Dick, I'm going to be a bride a real one. I told brother John and he sent me to Angel. I didn't come to you because I knew anything I wanted you'd let me have -- even if it were a husband. Guess who I'm engaged to?

Dick.

Alec Robinson.

Bess.

(Disappointed) Somebody told you. (Pointing) Now, Brother John, you've been telling him about it all this time.

John.

No, dear, we were speaking of something quite different.

Bess.

(To Dick) Well, Angel says when we are older, she sees no objection to our marriage. (Sighs) She thinks it will be about five years. My! that's a long time. But Alec's worth the delay. And I'm so happy. (Dreamily) Just to think what

it is to a young girl who loves some one with all her heart and soul, to have him take her to a nice little home -- all their own -- and call her his wife. (Feelingly) Oh! Dick, if you only knew what that means to a woman. Congratulate me.

Dick.

(Who has listened impassively, draws her to him)
I do little one. (Kisses her) I do.
(Bess goes to John, C )

John.

May no tears ever dim these little eyes except such as are shed in sympathy for those less fortunate than you are. God bless you! Darling, there --- run along with Angel.
(Bess goes out L.1.E. with Mrs. Van B. John approaches Dick who is still seated in chair and stands behind him)
To-night I have heard two confessions of love in this room --- one from Phyllis Lee, the other from our little Bess.
(At this moment Dick shows that his sisters words have moved him. John ovserves this and tenderly places his hand on Dick's shoulder)
Suppose some one dealt with our sister as you are dealing with Phyllis Lee?

Dick.

Oh God!
(Dick, with a cry of horror, starts to his feet, instinctivoly clinching his fists. Then with a sob falls back into the chair utterly broken.)

John.

If I have lost the power to plead with you, let her innocent tongue speak for me. Not as the man now, but as your brother once more, I beg, I implore, do what is right. Give me your hand. Be my brother Dick again.
(Dick slowly rises, goes to John and takes his outstretched hand.)
Give me that promise.

Dick

I do.

John.

You will make Phyllis Lee your wife.

Dick.

Yes.

John.

Not because I want you to, but because your heart turns of itself towards the woman over whose letter I found you that night with bowed head.

Dick.

Yes.

(John presses his hand and goes to the chapel door which he quietly opens. The low sobbing of a woman is heard. Listening.)

Phyllis'

John.

(Calling) Ann.

(Ann appears at door R.2.E. looks at John, reads the truth in his face then retires to the chapel. In a moment Phyllis appears)

Phyllis, my brother has something to say to you.

(He goes L. the firelight falling strongly on his face Ann appears at door R.2.E.)

(Phyllis has come forward R.C.)

Dick.

Phyllis is there love enough left in your heart for me, to forgive all the misery I have caused you?

(Phyllis turning to him wistfully)

Not yet, not yet. I could better bear your reproaches than what you are about to say. False to myself, false to those at home, false to you, I come with eyes open at last. Phyllis, I want you to be --- my wife.

Phyllis.

(Tearfully - Coming to him) Oh, Dick! You do love me then?

Dick.

Yes.

(Dick's head gently sinks upon her shoulder.)

John.

One thing more. She will return with Ann to-night. Let her bear your name.

Dick.

Whenever you will.

John.

Now.

Dick.

And the words that will make her --- my wife?

John.

(Approaching the table, placing his hand on the prayer book)

I -- will -- speak -- them.

-$- C U R T A I N -$-

-%- T H E   C H A R I T Y   B A L L -%-

A C T   I V.

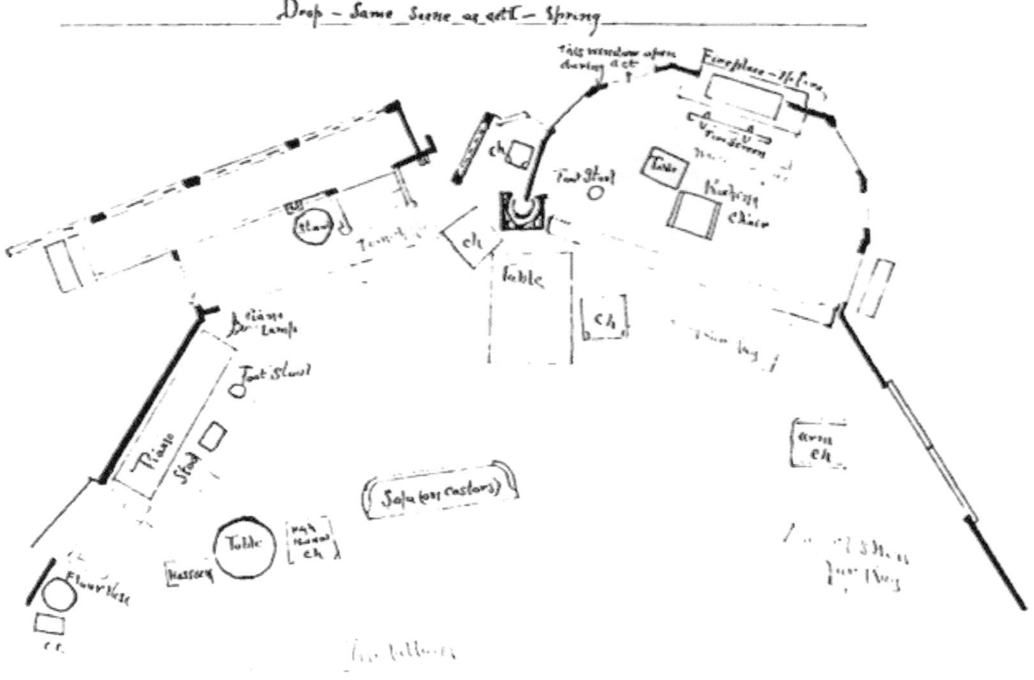


Act IV – Same set as act I

## PROPERTY PLOT --- A C T IV

Furniture, Same as Act I. Re-arranged as per Diagram.

Sofa down R. C. on Castors.
The lamp used by Betts in Act 1. on Mantel.
Large American flag in Window up L. C.
On Stand, in Alcove: Chess Board, Chess and Chess-box and a Newspaper.

----------

## SIDE PROPERTIES --- A C T IV.

Off R.: Package neatly done up, for Alec.
Large bundle consisting of many pasteboard boxes tied together for Bess.
Off L.: Small tray with Wreath of flowers, for Phyllis.

----------

## L I G H T S ------------ A C T IV.

Same lights used in same position as in Act I. EXCEPT Red Calcium down L. not used.

Red Mediums on Bunches A.B.C.D. Change gradually to BLUE on Cue "I hope you'll find it soon".

On same cue, Foots and Borders worked down to 1/2.

On cue "She's in love", White Calcium L. turned on. Remains till curtain.

Lanterns lighted by Jasper.

No fire in Fireplace.

House lights on 3/4 at rise of curtain. Down to 1/2 on "I Hope you'll find it soon."

---oOo---

# -%- THE CHARITY BALL -%-

## ACT IV.

SCENE:- The Sitting Room. Same scene as Act I. Afternoon of Memorial Day, 1889. Where the trees and vines in Act I. were bare, foliage is now seen through the windows. For arrangement of furniture see diagram. The rays of the setting sun come into the room through the open window.

DISCOVERED:- Betts Seated in Alcove up L., chess board on lap with chess. On stand by him lies a newspaper containing a chess problem, in which he is wrapt. Moving a piece he hums pleased, then takes back the piece and is silent while he ponders. Mrs. Van B. coming down stairs R.3.E.

Betts.

The most difficult problem I ever found in a newspaper, and I've been working the chess column for years.

Mrs. Van B.

Still on the problem, Mr. Betts?

Betts.

Joe Randolph and I work 'em out together and divide the prize. Joe makes his living at it.

Phyllis.

(Enters L.2.E. with wreath of cut flowers on tray; coming down)

Mother!

Mrs.Van B.

My daughter. After our drive, Bess and I called upon Ann. The steamer didn't reach quarantine till late last night, so she couldn't get home till this morning.

Phyllis.

She must be very anxious to see the Rectory once more.

Mrs.V.B.

I feel as if my own child had come back to me. Eighteen months since she went away -- two weeks after your marriage.

Phyllis.

Yes.

Mrs. V.B.

I shall never forget that night after the Charity Ball, when Ann came up to my room and told me that early next morning, Dick had to go away and that you and he had arranged to be married that night. To think that you and Dick loved each other, and I didn't know it. It was only after John pronounced you man and wife and Ann made everything clear to me, that I recovered from my surprise. But what detains Bess?

Phyllis.

Didn't she come in with you?

Mrs.V.B/

No. She went up to the corner to see Judge Knox's regiment pass by. She said the parade to-day was beautiful. Dick used to be her companion always on Memorial Day. My Boy!

Phyllis.

You were very proud of him were you not, Mother?

Mrs.V.B.

Yes, but that unconquerable spirit of his always caused me anxiety. He was always first in every undertaking, until the day he made the whole business acknowledge him its master.

Betts.

(Aside) And that night he dropped down on his office floor -- dead. (Continues his game.)

Phyllis.

A year and three months ago since he was taken from us.

Mrs.V.B.

(Feeling the flowers) Why, you've been cutting some flowers?

Phyllis.

I am making a wreath.

Mrs.V.B.

Every week has its Memorial Day for you. But though a whole nation mingles its tears to-day, it strews its flowers of hope; so let us keep in the sun light, not in the shadow.

Betts.

(With a sudden ejaculation) I've done it.

Mrs.V.B.

Solved the problem, Mr. Betts?

Betts.

(Gathering up the pieces; hat and chess board, and starting to go R.)

Exactly what I've done. Wager Joe Randolph hasn't come anywhere near it. I'll go show him how to do it.

(Chuckling)

Phyllis.

(X'ing to him) Mr. Betts you told me this morning you would postpone your visit to Woodlawn until the day had grown quiet.

Betts.

Yes.

Phyllis.

Will you see me before you go?

(Betts nods assent and with chessboard under his arm, exit C. humming, "See the conquering hero comes." Phyllis X's to piano and plays a low sweet air. Bess laughing runs on C. from R.)

Bess.

Judge Knox looks just magnificent on his big black charger in his Colonel's uniform. If I were the enemy -- well, I wouldn't have the heart to shoot a sight like that. Mrs. Knox passed him in her victoria. The Judge made his horse prance and saluted her; and she waived her handkerchief frantically. Ha - ha - ha! Such fun!

Phyllis.

Alec belongs to the same regiment, doesn't he?

Bess.

(Rising: with a sudden change of manner, her chin in the air)

You mean Mr. Robinson? I believe he does.

Mrs. V. B.

(Significantly) Mr. Robinson. Oh!

Phyllis.

There has been a little difficulty between you and -- Mr. Robinson?

Bess.

(With a toss of the head) An insurmountable difficulty. Angel and Phyllis, you will oblige me by not alluding to that person in my presence again.

Mrs.V.B.

Then you're not in the same frame of mind.

Bess.

No. The frame's broken.

(Goes up to the window in Alcove L. and takes in a large American flag which is supposed to be hanging over the window sill. Enter John from study R. 2. E.)

John.

Phyllis, was it you I saw in the conservatory just now?

Phyllis.

(Rising) Yes.

John.

I spoke to you, but you didn't answer.

Phyllis.

(Rising and taking flowers from top of piano where she has placed them.)
I was so intent on what I was doing that I didn't hear you.

John.

I'm glad to see you so contented -- your life so peaceful. It is a solace to us all. Go finish your wreath.

(Exit Phyllis L.2.E.)

Bess.

(Coming down with flag.) Halloo! Brother John. I have something to communicate to you.

John.

Indeed! What is it?

Bess.

It's off

John.

What is off?

John.

I suppose I shall have a call to-night from Alex. Mother, tell me about Ann.

Mrs. V. B.

Strange. Ann's first words after I kissed her were: "Tell me about John."

John.

Mother, since she went away as the days have gone by, I have missed her from her accustomed place. The world has seemed different to me. My work has been harder. Even the old Rectory became gloomy without her. But now that she has come back again -- Oh, mother, even you do not know what she has been to me.

Mrs. V.B.

My boy, because your mother cannot see, do you think all things are hidden from her?

John.

In every thought of my life I have some how placed you and her together.

Mrs. V. B.

While we have many friends, we have but one mother, and there is only one beside our mother, who can share a confidence like her.

John.

True.

(M U S I C   N O. 1 3)

Mrs. V. B.

(Rises: starts to go up to R.2.E. turns and comes down to John.)

You see at last, what I have known all along -- that between you and Ann the feeling is not friendship.

(Exit R.2.E.)

John.

No mother. Great as my love was for that poor child, above and beyond it there has been a love not unknown -- only misunderstood. But after what has passed between us, would she understand? Between us now there can be only friendship.

(Exit R.2.E. Enter Bess down steps R.3.E. with a large package.)

Bess.

I saw him coming up the street. (Places package on sofa R.) Now, Mr. Robinson, I'll make you think you're on a transatlantic steamer, with an iceberg very near you. Here he comes. I must compose myself. I'll pretend to be happy.

(X'ing to piano R.)

Of course there's no pretence about it, when I am happy.

(With broken voice)

very, very h-- happy.

(Singing song from "Mikado", "I am happy -- Oh so happy, always laughing nectar quaffing etc." Enter Elex. C. dressed as a private of Judge Knox's regiment. He also carries a package. He stands on the threshold.)

Alec.

(Dignified) Miss Van Buren!

Bess.

(Paying no attention - sings.) "I am happy -- Oh so happy."

Alec.

Miss Van Buren.

Bess.

(Stopping) Oh, Mr. Robinson. Pardon me. I was so occupied with my music. Will you walk in?

Alec.

Thank you. (Coming down L.)

Bess.

Did you call to see brother John or Angel?

Alec.

I called to see you.

Bess.

(Crossing to R. C. sitting on sofa. Formally.)

Oh! Be seated.

Alec.

You are very kind.

(BUS. Sits awkwardly on edge of chair holding package on his knees.)

Bess.

Shall I ring for a messenger to put your package on the table?

Alec.

You needn't trouble.

(Puts it on the floor. Short, awkward pause.)

Bess.

Very fine weather we are having.

Alec.

Very

(Short awkward pause)

Made the marching very pleasant to-day.

Bess.

Did you parade with the regiment to-day?

Alec.

Of course. Didn't you see me?

Bess.

(With a dignified shake of the head)

No.

(Alec appears crushed.)

As you remarked that you came to see me, will you kindly state the purpose of this interview?

Alec.

I should have called this morning, only I was obliged to take my place in the ranks.

Bess.

In the ranks -- Yes.

Alec.

(Hurt) If I am only in the ranks it is because --

Bess.

When Judge Knox married your aunt, he put you there.

Alec.

I am proud to acknowledge Judge Knox as my Colonel. There are worse soldiers than Uncle Pete.

Bess.

(With a significant look) Much worse.

Alec.

Miss Van Buren, your joking is ill timed. (Rising) We will conclude this interview.

Bess.

The sooner the quicker -- (Rising) I mean the better.

Alec.

(Placing his bundle on the table) I came to return your presents. They are in that box.

Bess.

(Taking her package and placing it on the table.)

This bundle contains yours. I had intended sending it. If you care to open the bundle and count them, you will find them all there. The only regret is that it is out of my power to return the Huyler's candy and the ice-cream sodas, with which you have favored me.

Alec.

Don't mention them. They are counterbalanced by the silk handkerchiefs which you have embroidered for me, and which, I am sorry to say, have been lost in the wash.

Bess.

Your letters are there. You may need them again. They will spare you the pain of composing. I couldn't find your last. When I do, I will mail it to you. It must have been mislaid.

Alec.

(Pointing to portion of envelope sticking out of the bosom of her dress.)

What's that?

Bess.

Oh! It must have slipped there -- by accident.

Alec.

I thought I recognized my envelope. That's my color.

Bess.

(Returning it) Crush Strawberry. How fitting.

Alec.

Now that this painful interview is over, I will take my leave.

(Goes up C. with hat.)

Bess.

(X'ing R. and seating herself at piano.)

I'm so happy -- Oh -- So happy.

Alec.

Of course you are aware that you are all wrong.

Bess.

(Turning on Piano stool)
Excuse me, I am aware of no such thing. The fault is all on your side.

Alec.

(With a polite bow)
I hope I am too much of a soldier to contradict a lady.
(Goes up C. and puts helmet on chair.)

Bess.

It's a pity you didn't have on your uniform last night when the difficulty happened.

Alec.

(Coming down) There's sure to be a row between somebody whenever Mrs. Homer G. Putnam has private theatricals for her waifs. You had no right to stand at the side with Jack Dexter and laugh at me going through my scene in "As you like it."

Bess.

(Rising and coming to C.) Jack Dexter asked me if I didn't think it was ridiculous for Mrs. Putnam to cast you for Charles, the Wrestler. When I saw you in that close fitting costume I couldn't help laughing. Everybody laughed.

Alec.

Jack Dexter thought it was ridiculous, did he? Why did'nt they get somebody else to play the part? I'm black and blue already from rehearsals. It may be Shakespeare's conception of the part to have Orlando throw the wrestler. I haven't said anything. But you just wait till the night of the performance. I'll make Jack Dexter sorry he ever played Orlando.
(Starting up stage.)
Good bye!

Bess.

(Unconsciously picks up a corner of the flag, swinging it to and fro nervously)
I hope, although we are about to part —
(With effort)
forever, that you will do nothing rash.

Alec.

(Taking up the other corner of the flag and swinging it nervously)
Oh, I don't care what becomes of me now. Nothing would please me better than for a war to break out to-night and me be ordered to the front.

Bess.

(Softening) But -- You might get shot.

Alec.

(Carelessly) Oh yes! Five or six bullets in me now, wouldn't make much difference.

Bess.

Although you are nothing to me any longer, I shouldn't like to hear of such an accident happening to you.

Alec.

I suppose when the tidings came, you would go to the piano and sing --

(Singing in broken voice)

"I'm so happy -- Oh! So happy."

(Turns away affected.)

Bess.

(Tearfully) N--n--no I wouldn't Alec.

Alec.

Y--y--yes you would, Bess.

Bess.

(Xing L. still retaining end of flag.)

You see if I will.

Alec.

(Starting to go up stage, still retaining end of flag.)

Farewell, Miss Van Buren.

Bess.

(Pulling him back) You seem to be in a terrible hurry to go, Mr. Robinson.

Alec.

I don't think this agony is good for us.

Bess.

(Getting up to sofa R. C. Sniffling.)

No --

Alec.

One last word. If you are ever in need, and want a friend come to me.

Bess.

Oh! Alec, you are so noble!

Alec.

Farewell.

Bess.

G— good bye.

Alec.

Another last word. When I find somebody else to take your place --

(Bess begins to cry.)

though I may give her my hand, my heart belongs to you.

(She puts her head on his shoulder, sobbing. During the above they have gradually enveloped themselves in the flag. In their efforts to wipe away their tears with the corners of the flag, they bring it over their heads and sit precipitately upon the sofa entirely concealed under the folds of the flag.

Enter Judge Knox C. - dressed as a Colonel of the National guard.)

Judge.

Is my wife here? She promised to come with a carriage and take me home -- and my wife never forgets.

(Absently places his helmet on Alec's head, and comes down C. Bess and Alec push sofa back.)

Cruger never forgets me either. I met Cruger to-day and he indulged in one of his Stock Exchange jokes. He said if my horse and I were done in bronze we'd make a splendid equestrian statue for the Old Ladies' Home.

(Xing R.)

I'll get even with Cruger for that yet.

(Opens door R. I. E.)

Ah, there she is!

(Alec and Bess still enveloped in the flag, rise, with the Judge's hat on top of them and cross the room, to the alcove sitting in the rocking chair.)

My heart fairly flutters at the sight of her. Coming sweetheart.

(Turns to get his hat and is amazed at finding it gone - Looks around room.)

I could have sworn I left my hat there.

(Seeing it in alcove -- startled.)

How the devil did it get up there?

(Alec and Bess rock violently. The Judge watching the movement dumbfounded)

Eh?

(Goes R. and calls)

Sweetheart! Sweetheart!

(Enter Mrs. Knox - formerly Mrs De Peyster - followed by Mrs. Van Buren.)

Mrs.K.

Peter dear, what's the matter?

Judge.

Look into my eyes. Are my pupils dilated? Do you notice any incipient traces of insanity about me?

Mrs.K.

Why, Peter!

Judge.

I placed my hat there. Then I found it there, and saw it move there.

(Bess and Alec rock again.)

Mrs.K.

Good gracious! There's something under the flag.

(Judge goes up C., throws back the top of the flag, discovers Alec and Bess in the act of kissing, unconscious of everything around them. Bess gives a slight cry. They rise quickly and stand with flag partially around them.)

Judge.

There are two somethings.

Mrs.K.

Alec!

Alec.

We claim the protection of our country's flag.

Mrs.V.B.

What are you doing, Bess?

Bess.

Standing by the flag, Angel.

Alec.

We were only looking for a quiet spot.

Judge.

Well, I hope you'll find it soon --

(L I G H T S  G O  DOWN)

for your methods are not only original, but decidedly outre.

Bess.

Please excuse us. We didn't hear anybody come in.

Mrs.V.B.
Then you have patched up your little difficulty?

Bess.
(Bus. with flag.) Yes, we are in the same frame again.

Judge.
And a very pretty chromo you make.
(Bess comes to Mrs. V.B.)
Young man, does your financial condition warrant your assuming the responsibility of paying this young woman's board bills for the balance of the term of your natural existence?

Alec.
Now Uncle Pete, don't joke, I don't like jokes.

Judge.
What's that?

Mrs.K.
Quite true, Peter, Alec could never bear to receive or play a joke.

Judge.
I think, sweetheart, that you do our nephew a great injustice I think that with his sense of humor he would not be averse to a joke --- if it were a corking good one.
(Alec laughs - Bess starts to take package from table.)

Alec.
I'll carry them, Bess.
(Going to stairs R.3.E. with packages.)
I mean to carry your burdens all through life.

Bess.
(Apart) Alec, I'll sort all your letters over again and tie them all up with fresh ribbon.
(Exeunt Bess and Alec R.3.E. upstairs.)

Mrs. Van B.
Judge, did you have a hard day's march?

Judge.
A hard day's ride. They sent me a car horse to parade on. Every time my sword clanked he thought it was the car bell and stopped. Nothing would induce him to go on but clanking it again.

Mrs.K.
I hope Darling, you were in no danger on such an animal.

Judge.

Your Darling hasn't been so shaken up since he went to Chicago on the B. & O. The next time I parade, I'll go down to Chambers Street and get a horse out of a harness store.

Mrs.V.B.

Let me get you a cup of tea, Judge. It will refresh you.

Mrs.K.

Yes, Peter do. Nothing restores the tissue like tea.

Judge.

Very well! My four hours on that Arabian steed have caused a desire for something soothing. (Aside) I'll stand up and take a little tea.

Mrs.K.

I'll go with you dear. I know just how he likes it.

Mrs.V.B.

One year yesterday since you were married.

Judge.

I'd like to begin with yesterday and live it backward. You don't mind a couple of old spoons, do you?

Mrs.V.B.

Old spoons? No. It is a part of the family silver that we ought never to permit to grow tarnished.

Mrs.K.

Our occasional little rubs only serve to make brighter this piece of precious metal.

Judge.

(Playfully) Oh, go along now. (To Mrs. V.B.) There is only one thing that mars our otherwise harmonious career.

Mrs.K.

Indeed, what is it, dear?

Judge.

That's the parrot. I am awakened every morning by that parrot's screeching, "De Peyster, De Peyster, it's time to get up." Good Heavens! suppose De Peyster should get up.

(Mrs.K. is much shocked)

My dear, I wish you would teach that bird that I am not De Peyster.

(Enter Jasper R.2:E. lights piano lamp, gets flag, puts sofa down stage - lights three lamps in alcove and exits L.2.E.)

Mrs.K.

Very well, Peter, Polly shall go into another room.

Judge.

(Aside) If it don't, I'l give Polly a powder and turn Polly into a bird of Paradise.

(Exeunt Mrs. Van S. and Mrs.K. R.I.E. Enter John R.2.E.)

Ah! John-- have you seen Ann?

John.

Not yet.

Judge.

I'm glad of that I want to ask your help in a matter that concerns her deeply. I'm her god-father, you know, and ever since she was a little child she has poured out her troubles to me. Now I've discovered that she's in love.

John.

Ann!

Judge.

Cupid has fired into her heart everything he had -- quiver and all. I've had some experience myself and I know what I'm talking about.

John.

Who is it Ann Loves?

Judge.

I prefer to keep his name to myself for the present- she went away on his account-- some misunderstanding.

John.

Misunderstanding?

Judge.

Now of course John there's nothing that would please you and I so much as to see Ann happily married-

John.

She would be happy with him?

Judge.

Oh, the man loves her.

(John turns away slightly)

I never felt so positive of it as I do at the present moment.

(W A R N M U S I C)

Judge.

Now you talk to her John- make her tell you the truth, the whole truth, I think you'll marry her soon.
(Exit R.I.E.)

(M U S I C)

John.

Ann has given her love to some one. She will become a wife. Well, she will be happy. And her husband-- whoever he may be, he must be happy in her love-- Oh! Ann in this the bitterest loss of my life, I shall be without your help. I must suffer alone.
(He falls into a chair, his head upon his arms on the table.
Ann, who has passed the window on the landing, is coming down the steps R.3.E. then she descends.)

Ann

John!

John.

(Starts, rises and takes her hands)
Ann! Ann!

Ann.

I'm-- I'm so glad to see you, John!
(Pressing her hand to her face for a moment as though a little faint.)
I declare the happiness of being home again is harder to withstend thean the sorrow of parting. John, I just passed the old window seat where we used to sit and read to-gether and, I know you'll think me foolish, John, but before coming down to you I sat there and had a good cry.

John.

Ah! then you were glad to get back to the old Rectory, weren't you?

Ann.

Glad! Why just now I stole into the house on purpose that nobody might know I was here so I could go to every familiar nook and corner and say "how de do" to them all, after being away from them so long.

John.

They have missed you.

Ann.

And I have missed them. Not a day went by-- not an hour, that my thought didn't turn from the scenes through which I was passing to the old Rectory of St. Mildred-- and my heart never failed to follow my thoughts. Ah! it is over a year since I said good bye to the dear old place.

John.

Ann, you went away with trouble at your heart of which you told me nothing.

Ann.

John!

John.

I have learned it from others.

Ann.

Learned what?

John.

That you went away because of a misunderstanding between you and some one you love.

(Ann sits R.C.)

Let me hear it from your own lips that I may be sure.

Ann.

(Agitated) I-- I cannot speak of it to you.

John.

I may be able to help you.

Ann.

My love is hopeless.

John.

Then there is someone that you love?

Ann.

(Lowering her eyes) Yes.

John.

Who loves you?

Ann.

No!

John.

You went away to avoid him?

Ann.

Yes, yes.

John.

You love him so much?

Ann.

(Going to C.) More than he will ever know.

John.

Ann, do you think I will let a misunderstanding keep you from the man you love when I know that he loves you. Judge Knox told me so. He told me to come to you. (Earnestly) And do you think he would let me speak to you unless he were sure?

Ann.

I— I don't know. I never in my life was quite so perplexed.
(Everybody to end the act)

John.

Ann, it was in this very room, over this table, just as we are now, that I told you of a love that seemed to promise happiness. Don't shut me out of your happiness. Let me be to you now what you were then to me. Do you remember when we read together the story of David Copperfield? How the friendship between Agnes and David hid from them their love for each other?

Ann.

Not from Agnes.

John.

True, it was only David who was deceived. And like him I have been blind. My love for Phyllis was like David's love for Dora. With that love I still had the friendship and sympathy of one who was to me as a sister. When Phyllis passed out of my life, I still had that friendship and sympathy and I could endure. It was only when Agnes was taken from me, that I realized what she had been to me.

Ann.

(Rising) Then why not go to her and tell her.

John.

(Rising) It is too late.

Ann.

So David thought when he spoke to Agnes.

John.

But the woman I love, loves someone else.

Ann.

Are you sure?

John.

Yes, Ann, for it is you!

(W A R N   C H I M E S)

Ann.

John!

John.

This should never have passed my lips did I not wish you to know how dear your happiness is to me. Tell me your secret as I have told you mine.

Ann.

Oh, John, spare me - I'm not myself.

John.

But you will tell me; you will let me help you?

Ann.

You do help me John, have you forgotten that the feelings of Agnes were for David? When he questioned her about the man she loved, he found it was himself.

John.

Ann!

Ann.

Now do you know why I had to go away.

John.

Ann - Ann - do you love me?

(C H I M E S - STOP MUSIC)

Ann.

Yes.

(They embrace.)

(CHIMES ARE HEARD)

(Enter Judge Knox R.I.E.)

(R I N G   M U S I C)

(W A R N   C U R T A I N)

Judge.

John- did she tell you?

John.

Yes.

(Enter Mrs. Van Buren and Mrs. Knox R. I. E.)

Judge.

Sweetheart, a word in your ear.
(Speaks apart with Mrs. K. and Mrs. Van B.)
(Bess runs on R.3.E. followed by Alec - Phyllis enters from the alcove with the wreath of flowers which she gives to Betts.)

Betts.

Brother John, it isn't off! It's on again for keeps.
(Bess and Alec go up the stairs and talk confidentially John comes down toward ANN.)

Ann.

John, shall I tell you my secret now?

John.

Yes.

Ann.

I have loved you all my life.

(R I N G M U S I C)

(R I N G C U R T A I N)

(Bess seen through the window on the landing with Alec, Judge and Mrs. Knox watching John and Ann, the Judge speaking of them to Mrs. Van B. who listens pleased. Betts has left Phyllis and stands with the weath on the threshold at the back to take his departure. Phyllis has placed the lamp used in Acts I. and III. on the table in the alcove and is in the act of lighting it as the chimes ring out and the curtain slowly descends.)

-%- C U R T A I N -%-

---oOo---

(N)

www.ingramcontent.com/pod-product-compliance
Lightning Source LLC
Chambersburg PA
CBHW021049030726
47496CB00006B/1763
* 9 7 8 3 7 4 4 7 8 1 6 1 9 *